ALSO BY TINA FOLSOM

Prequel Novella: Mortal Wish
Samson's Lovely Mortal (Scanguards Vampires, Book 1)
Amaury's Hellion (Scanguards Vampires, Book 2)
Gabriel's Mate (Scanguards Vampires, Book 3)
Yvette's Haven (Scanguards Vampires, Book 4)
Zane's Redemption (Scanguards Vampires, Book 5)
Quinn's Undying Rose (Scanguards Vampires, Book 6)
Oliver's Hunger (Scanguards Vampires, Book 7)
Thomas's Choice (Scanguards Vampires, Book 8)
Silent Bite (Scanguards Vampires, Book 8 1/2)
Cain's Identity (Scanguards Vampires, Book 9)
Luther's Return (Scanguards Vampires – Book 10)
Blake's Pursuit (Scanguards vampires – Book 11)
Fateful Reunion (Scanguards Vampires – Book 11 1/2)

Lover Uncloaked (Stealth Guardians – Book 1)
Master Unchained (Stealth Guardians – Book 2)

A Touch of Greek (Out of Olympus – Book 1)
A Scent of Greek (Out of Olympus – Book 2)
A Taste of Greek (Out of Olympus – Book 3)
A Hush of Greek (Out of Olympus – Book 4)

Lawful Escort
Lawful Lover
Lawful Wife
One Foolish Night
One Long Embrace
One Sizzling Touch

Venice Vampyr

Fateful Reunion is a work of fiction. Names, characters, places, and incidents are the products of the author's imagination and are used fictitiously. Any resemblance to actual events, locales, or persons, living or dead, is entirely coincidental.

2016 Tina Folsom

Published in the United States

Cover design: Leah Kaye Suttle
Cover photo: Bigstockphoto.com

Printed in the United States of America

FATEFUL REUNION

SCANGUARDS VAMPIRES #11 1/2

TINA FOLSOM

1

It wasn't busy in the V lounge, where Scanguards employees liked to relax in between their shifts, catch up with their colleagues, and enjoy a free glass of blood. And that was just what Roxanne needed now. Something to take the edge off after an awfully boring eight-hour patrol through Laurel Heights, where absolutely nothing had happened. Patrols like that made her uneasy, made her feel almost as if she'd overlooked something.

She'd much rather deal with a few criminals, set them straight by scaring the shit out of them, than wander the streets without any incident. When she dealt with criminals and made sure they didn't hurt anybody, she felt she had a purpose. That's why she'd signed up to be a bodyguard in the first place.

If only Gabriel Giles, her boss and second-in-command at Scanguards, would give her a decent assignment, but apparently it was slow right now. No conventions in town, no VIP visits, no threats. And therefore no extra clients to protect, which meant every bodyguard who was not on client detail was patrolling.

And she'd drawn the short straw and been assigned to one of the safest neighborhoods, while younger, less experienced bodyguards had gotten the juicy neighborhoods like SOMA or the Bayview, neighborhoods where action was guaranteed. But no, Amaury's twins, both still in training, had been assigned to those neighborhoods, chaperoned by fully-fledged bodyguards like John and Haven. If that wasn't nepotism at work, then she didn't know what was.

Still grumbling to herself, she ordered a glass of O-Neg at the bar and looked around, when she saw Thomas gesturing her to join him in the comfortable sitting area in front of the fireplace. Oliver, who was sitting opposite him in an armchair, looked over his shoulder.

"Hey, Roxanne," Oliver greeted her.

She snatched the glass of blood from the bar, nodded thanks to the bartender, and walked over to the two men. She'd always liked Thomas, the passionate biker and IT genius, who ran the IT operations of the company together with his mate Eddie.

"Hey guys," she greeted them, stepping close to the armchairs. "What are you up to?"

"We were just talking about Wesley," Thomas said with a smile.

She shrugged. Wesley wasn't exactly her favorite Scanguards employee. And the fact that he was gone suited her just fine. "Hmm."

Seemingly oblivious to her disinterest in the subject, Oliver said, "I hope he's alright. Honestly, I wish Samson had insisted that he take one of us with him for protection. We have no idea what we're dealing with when it comes to these Stealth Guardians. Nobody knows who they are."

"Haven and Wesley did as much research on them as they could. But there wasn't much," Thomas admitted. "All we know is that they are preternatural creatures, and that they can somehow travel through portals."

"Like wormholes?" Oliver asked.

Thomas shrugged. "Kind of. And who knows what other skills they have."

"If they mean us well, they could be of use. After all, the guy Wesley chased after didn't interfere when we took out those rogue vampires, nor did he attack us," Oliver said. "Still, I wish he would have taken one of us with him for protection."

Roxanne scoffed. "I'm with Samson. Why waste a perfectly good vampire to protect a witch?"

Thomas raised an eyebrow. "I had no idea you didn't like Wes. He sure likes you."

She'd noticed that, too, but had done her best to keep him at arm's length. Her jaw tightened. "I've got nothing against him personally."

"Personally?" Thomas asked. "I mean, I know that vampires and witches are sworn enemies. Old feuds and all that. But it's different at Scanguards, and I thought you knew that. In the end it was just prejudice that started those feuds. It's history. We're above all that."

Roxanne swallowed, knowing that Thomas of all people knew about prejudice, because he'd been at the receiving end of it when he'd been a young man in Victorian England, shunned for being gay.

But her dislike of witches didn't stem from prejudice. She wished it did. Then her heart wouldn't bleed anew every time she was confronted with one and reminded of her past. However, this was nobody's business, but her own.

"Well, I'm not gonna miss him if he doesn't come back."

Oliver gave a light shake of his head. "Don't you think that's a little harsh?" He exchanged a look with Thomas, before he continued, "Don't get me wrong, Wes rubbed me the wrong way more than once, and we've had our fights, but he's a good guy. When it comes down to it, he'll have your back."

An icy hand clamped around her heart and squeezed it to the point of pain. "You can never trust a witch, no matter what he promises." *No matter how much he claims he loves you.*

"I'm sorry to hear that, Roxanne," Thomas said, a contemplative expression on his face. He ran a hand through his blond hair. "If you want to—"

The beeping of her cell phone saved her. "Excuse me." She pulled it from her pocket and glanced at it, sighing in relief when she read the text message. "Gabriel needs me. See you guys later."

She practically raced out of the V lounge, leaving her untouched glass of blood on a table near the exit. Once in the hallway, she took the elevator to the third floor where new clients were welcomed. When she stepped out of it, she nearly collided with Gabriel who was coming from the other end of the corridor where the stairs were located.

"Oh, there you are," he said, nodding.

"You made it sound important."

"I think it is." The large scar that graced his face from ear to chin seemed to throb. His ponytail of thick dark-brown hair was tied low at his nape. He motioned to the door of one of the small conference rooms. "I need a woman's intuition."

Roxanne sighed. Great, so this wasn't about her taking on a new client. This was about her advising Gabriel. Pushing her disappointment back, she said, "For what?"

"We got approached by a potential client. He's not saying much, other than that he wants protection. He's requesting four bodyguards and requires that at least one of them be a female."

"Four? Who is he? The President of the United States?" she joked. Even prominent politicians rarely got more than two bodyguards assigned to them, unless a credible threat against them existed.

Gabriel didn't laugh. "I have no idea who he is. Or where he came from. Eddie ran his profile through the system already…"

"And?"

"Nothing. Absolutely nothing. As if he doesn't even exist."

"Well, if he doesn't exist, I don't see why he needs protection." She threw a few strands of her long auburn hair behind her shoulder.

"You've got your answer. Turn him down. So if that was all you needed, I'll see you later."

"That's not why I asked you up here."

Roxanne arrested her movement and lifted an eyebrow. "What then?"

Gabriel pointed to the door. "I want you to join me while I interview him further. Figure him out, you know."

"Since when do you need me to figure out a client?"

"Well, I would normally ask Wesley to sit in on this one, given the circumstances." He shrugged. "But since Wes has decided to chase after ghosts, I figured the next best person is a woman with an intuition as sharp as a knife's blade."

At his compliment, Roxanne felt her chest fill with pride. She was valued here at Scanguards. Respected. It was something that had eluded her in the past. But all that was behind her. She'd started a new life, far away from her old one. If only she could bury her past once and for all, she'd be happy, but despite the many years that had passed, certain memories kept resurfacing.

"Ready then?"

Gabriel's voice jolted her from her thoughts.

"Sure, lead the way."

Her boss opened the door to the conference room and walked inside. She followed and let her eyes roam. A man stood with his back to them, staring out through the window into the dark night. Roxanne pulled the door shut behind her and inhaled, recognizing one thing immediately: the man wasn't human, nor was he a vampire. He was a witch. No wonder Gabriel had wanted Wesley to be here. Now she understood. Apparently, even Gabriel didn't fully trust a witch.

"Mr. Dubois," Gabriel prompted. "Shall we continue our talk?"

"I was just admiring the view," the tall stranger said, turning. "Let's—" His gaze drifted to her and his words died.

As did everything inside Roxanne. Her heart stopped, her breath rushed from her lungs, and all the blood froze in her veins as if she'd fallen into a vat of liquid nitrogen. Maybe that scenario would have been the better option, rather than having to face *him*. Rather than having her heart broken once more.

"Charles." The word made its way past her paralyzed lips, squeezed out by the last breath of air her body was trying to hold on to.

2

"Roxanne."

He'd been preparing himself for this moment ever since he'd found out where she was living now, but still the sight of her caught him off guard.

Seeing her was like a dream, just like the many dreams he'd had of seeing her again, of once more gazing into her gray eyes and being under her spell. Because even vampires could cast spells. Roxanne had done so twenty-three years ago and captured him body and soul, spoiled him for every other woman, and made him regret what he'd done every single day and night. What he'd had to do, so they would all be safe.

Purposely, he hadn't searched for her after that fateful night when he'd had to leave her. Fate had dropped a responsibility into his lap that he couldn't shirk. But soon, he would be absolved of his duty and free again. Soon, he could try to redeem himself in Roxanne's eyes and hope she would forgive him.

Roxanne looked exactly how he remembered her. Her auburn hair still hung down past her shoulders, and would caress her nipples when she was naked. Her red lips were full and plump, beckoning him for a kiss. Her long legs were encased in tight black pants, accentuating their length. He remembered all too vividly, how she'd slung those legs around him and urged him to take her harder. Her vampire strength had been the biggest turn-on he'd ever experienced. But despite Roxanne's overwhelming physical power, they'd always been equals. All because in his arms she'd turned soft and yielding, and had purred like a tame kitten whenever he'd brought her to climax. Those had been the moments when he'd seen into her soul and realized that he'd never be free of her. She'd stolen his heart.

Only now, that same heart was in danger of being ripped out of his chest, if the furious look in Roxanne's eyes was anything to go by.

"I see introductions aren't necessary." An implied question colored the Scanguards boss's voice.

But Charles wasn't going to air his dirty laundry in front of a vampire he'd met only a half hour earlier. This was between him and Roxanne. Between him and the love of his life.

Charles opened his mouth, but he didn't get a chance to say anything.

"How dare you show up here?"

It wasn't exactly a warm welcome, not that he could blame her. But to hear such fury in Roxanne's voice and see her eyes glaring red as she stalked toward him in single-minded determination meant that time hadn't healed the wound he'd left behind.

"You rotten, devious, no-good, lying witch! And to think that I trusted you once!" Her eyes narrowed on him at the same time as her fangs lengthened and peeked from between her parted lips.

His pulse kicked up, doubling the rate at which his heart beat, though his reaction wasn't borne out of fear. He'd always enjoyed her bite, always loved the special connection he felt to her when she lodged her fangs in his neck and drank from him. Even now, as she approached, pure hatred spewing from her every pore, he couldn't suppress the shiver that raced down his spine at the thought of feeling her fangs in his flesh one last time. And if he hadn't sworn to uphold his promise and fulfill his duty, he would let it happen. But too much was at stake, so dying in her arms and paying for what he'd done to her wasn't an option.

He raised his hand and sent a blast of air in her direction, stopping her approach. Roxanne was jerked back by the sudden barrier he'd thrown up.

"Don't do anything you'll regret, Roxanne," he cautioned.

"I'm not going to regret ripping you to pieces, you bastard!" she ground out and pushed against the barrier.

"What the fuck is this?" Gabriel interrupted. "I want an explanation. Now!"

Charles glanced at the scarred vampire. "It has nothing to do with Scanguards or with my request for protection."

Roxanne scoffed. "You've got that right. You're the last person Scanguards would ever agree to protect. You're not worth it! I hope whomever you're running from gets to you and makes you suffer." Her jaw clenched, as if she was holding on to the last vestiges of her control.

"Don't you think that's a little harsh, darling?"

She jumped at him then, and this time, his concentration slipped, and the barrier he'd thrown up crumbled—or maybe he let it crumble. Roxanne broke through and slammed him against the window with such force that he was surprised it didn't break or at least crack. Bullet-proof, he registered briefly, before Roxanne lifted him up and threw him clear across the room where he flew into the wall, leaving a dent in it, before crashing down to the floor.

She charged at him again, but didn't get far. Her boss snatched her from behind and stopped her from doing any more damage.

"That's enough, Roxanne!" Gabriel ordered, keeping a firm grip on her bicep.

Her head snapped to her boss, and now she directed her anger at him. "You can't take him on as a client. He's bad news. Whatever he tells you is going to be a lie. Don't trust him."

"We'll see about that." Gabriel motioned to him. "What have you got to say, Mr. Dubois?"

"His name isn't Dubois," Roxanne interrupted. "And he needs no protection. Do you, *darling*?"

Her last word was a pure snarl, though a tiny ray of hope dared to bloom in his chest—a chest that ached now as he tried to get up. Involuntarily, he groaned and braced himself against the wall. From what he could tell, he'd broken a rib or two, maybe three. Nothing a little healing spell wouldn't fix later.

Charles lifted his hand. "I'm just glad you haven't lost your touch, *darling*." He looked at Gabriel. "And don't worry, I have no intention of suing your company for assault." He lifted one corner of his mouth, trying for a nonchalant smile. "As you can see, Mr. Giles, I am indeed in need of your services. One never knows where the next attack will come from."

Roxanne growled like a caged beast. And damn it, what a turn-on that was. He was one sick son of a bitch to crave more abuse at her hands. Was he that starved for her touch that he'd even accept a beating from her, just to feel her hands on him again?

"Stand down, Roxanne," Gabriel ordered, casting a stern look at her.

"You're not going to listen to this bastard, are you?" She shook her head, disbelief spreading on her face. "You can't be serious! You asked me for my opinion. I've given it to you. He's rotten to the core. Don't get involved with him. You'll only regret it. We all will."

"Maybe we can discuss this in a more civilized manner," Gabriel suggested, though he was gritting his teeth, apparently not as calm as he pretended to be.

Roxanne braced her hands on her hips. "There's nothing to discuss."

"Clearly there's a lot to discuss," Gabriel suggested.

"Mr. Giles," Charles cut in. "I can assure you that despite the fact that Roxanne and I don't exactly get along these days—"

"I'd call that an understatement," Gabriel interrupted casually.

"Be that as it may, I've come here only to seek your services. I have no intention of harming any of you."

"Liar!" Roxanne glared at him, then addressed her boss directly. "If you take him on as a client, then I—"

"Roxanne!" Gabriel warned.

But her boss should have known better. Hell, even after twenty-three years Charles still knew her better than anybody else. Roxanne had been told one too many times by men what to do or not to do. And he could see it in her now: she was about to snap.

"I quit!"

Ah, shit! He'd expected her to do something rash, but to quit? Because of him? That wasn't part of the plan.

"You can't just quit!" Gabriel ground out. "Wait in my office for me. We'll talk."

"I've got nothing to say!" Roxanne yelled and charged to the door. She ripped it open. "I'm done with this!" She stormed out, slamming the door behind her so hard that the glass bowl on the conference table rattled.

For several moments, it was silent in the conference room. Charles closed his eyes, taking a deep breath. With it, his lungs expanded and pressed against his ribs, shooting pain through his chest.

"Fuck!"

Gabriel took a few steps toward him, but Charles lifted his hand. "I'm fine. It's just a few broken ribs." He forced a smile. "Though I wouldn't mind continuing our conversation sitting down."

Gabriel motioned to a chair.

Gratefully, Charles lowered himself to sit and watched his host do the same.

"You're not going to tell me what this was about, are you?" Gabriel asked.

He took his time answering. "No."

"Thought so. So how can I help you?"

"As I said, I'd like four bodyguards. And I'd like one of them to be Roxanne." That part was crucial. It was the only way he could force her to be in his presence and give him the opportunity to mend old wounds.

"Maybe your hearing got damaged when Roxanne threw you against the wall, because you obviously didn't hear that she just quit."

Charles chuckled. "Then you don't know Roxanne very well."

The Scanguards boss lifted an eyebrow and folded his hands. "Enlighten me."

Charles jerked his thumb toward the door. "That was just her way of telling me that she still loves me."

"Hmm. I think it's time I called my wife to tend to your medical needs. It appears you've got a concussion in addition to those broken ribs."

"Believe me, Mr. Giles, there's nothing wrong with my brain."

Though he couldn't say the same for his mind—which he'd clearly lost.

3

Twenty-three years earlier

Roxanne cast another look down the hotel corridor, first left then right. It was empty. Then she knocked at the door. It swung open instantly, and Charles pulled her into the room, shutting the door behind her.

His lips were on hers a moment later, kissing her with the same longing that she'd tried to keep contained during the long nights they'd been apart. She slung her arms around him and felt possessiveness surge through her, despite the fact that what they were doing was wrong. Wrong on so many levels. Because a vampire should never love a witch. But she couldn't command her heart to stop loving him, no matter the consequences. Charles embodied everything she'd ever wanted in a man: strength, integrity, and kindness.

When Charles finally released her lips, they were both breathing hard.

He pressed his forehead to hers. "Did anybody see you?"

"I was careful. I waited until Silas left with his men." She shuddered internally, knowing all too well that whenever Silas and his motley crew of sadistic vampires left the compound, they did so to wreak havoc. And she was caught in the middle.

"Good."

"But I don't have much time." She had to be back before the men returned and noticed her gone, or Silas would smell a rat and assign somebody to keep an eye on her.

"I know, baby," Charles murmured and busied himself with shoving her top up and pulling it over her head. Cool air blew against her heated skin, providing much needed relief. "But I need you. It's been too long."

Roxanne was already unbuttoning his shirt, not wanting to lose time either. They'd only ever had these stolen moments and knew how to make the most of it.

It only took a few seconds until they were both naked. Charles maneuvered them to the large bed which had already been turned down.

When Roxanne felt the soft sheets beneath her back and Charles's naked body on top of her, she sighed in contentment.

She loved his well-toned physique, his lean torso, his muscled thighs. And his face framed by short, dark hair, his strong jaw, full lips, and straight nose. But most of all she loved his chocolate-colored eyes. They signified everything good about him: he was a man of honor.

"Charles, I need you," she murmured against his neck. "Please take me."

He lifted his head and brushed his fingers through her hair. "I need you just as much. But I won't rush it. You deserve better. Damn, you deserve so much better than that animal—"

She pressed a finger to his lips. "Let's not talk about him. You know I can't break up with him. I know too much about his operations. He can't afford to let me live."

Pain lit up in Charles's eyes. Then one of the bedside lamps blew out.

"Charles!" she urged him, knowing his power had been the culprit. She'd never been afraid of it, though she had no defense against it. "Please, you've got to stay in control." Or they might draw attention to themselves. And that was something they couldn't afford. It was one of the reasons they always met at different places, never at Charles's home for fear that one day somebody might follow her.

"How can I?" he ground out. "When you're with him, I fear for your life. Don't you understand what it does to me?" He rolled off her and stared at the ceiling. "We can't go on like this any longer."

She sat up with a start. "Are you telling me you're leaving me?" A sob worked its way up her chest, but before it could roll over her lips, Charles had reared up and gripped her shoulders.

"Why would you think that? How could I ever leave you? I love you, Roxanne! More than life itself."

Though the words were a relief, his stormy facial expression didn't help ease her worries. "Then what?"

"We have to go away. Together."

"But he won't let me go."

"You're not going to ask for permission."

"He'll chase me."

"Not if he thinks you're dead."

Her heartbeat accelerated. "Oh my God, what are you planning?"

He cupped her cheek and stroked it, looking deep into her eyes. "I've thought it all through. It's the only way for us to be together. We have to stage your death."

"But how?"

"Two nights from now, I'll make sure Silas gets word from an informant that there's easy prey waiting for him. He and his men will leave the compound. That's when you'll act."

Roxanne bit her lip, worry charging through her. To cross an evil man like Silas was akin to signing her own death sentence. "If anything goes wrong, he'll hunt me down like a dog. I should just kill him."

"No!" Charles nearly yelled the word. "Even if you're able to kill him, his men will slaughter you. You'll never get out of there alive. I won't let you do it. I'd rather go in there myself and kill him."

Tears welled up in her eyes. "You know you won't get close enough. His men will sense you, despite your power, or maybe because of it. They'll have the upper hand. They'll kill you just because they can. And if they do that, you know I won't remain idle. You know I'll try to stop them. And then we'll both die. We'll never get away alive if we try to kill Silas."

"Then we have no other choice. We have to make sure Silas thinks you're dead. We'll make sure your death is believable. Since a vampire doesn't leave a body behind, but only dust, it'll be simple. Take your jewelry off and drop it to the floor in your room, together with your cell phone. Make it look like there was a break-in. Leave a stake on the ground, and sprinkle dust in the same spot."

"He'll never believe it. The compound is secure. Nobody can get in. Silas made sure of that."

Charles shook his head and stood up, reaching for his jacket, which was draped over the only armchair in the room. "If there's evidence of witchcraft, Silas will think a witch used a spell to get inside and kill you." He pulled an amulet out of the inside pocket and showed it to her.

"What is it?"

"It's a witch's protection stone. Many witches carry them. Tear it off the leather string and toss it on the floor in your room. Make it look like you were fighting a witch. When Silas finds it, he'll have proof that you were killed by a witch. He won't try to find you. He'll be too busy getting revenge on the witches."

"But won't that endanger every witch in this city?"

Charles sighed and laid the amulet on the bedside table before joining her on the bed again. "There's already open war between the vampires and the witches. This won't change anything. It won't make relations between the two species any more strained than they already are. What it will do, is free you. You know that. Deep down you know that this is our only chance. We can't expect help from my fellow witches. They would never accept you. They'd kill you on sight. We're on our own. Just you and me."

"Are you really prepared to give all this up for me?"

He smiled. "Oh, Roxanne, what would I be giving up? You know I'm not part of a coven. I've never liked their draconian rules and their preconceived ideas of who's good and who's bad. Look at us." He slid his hand under her chin, stroking her jaw with his thumb. "Haven't we proven that there needn't be war and hatred between our species? Haven't we proven that there can be love?"

Tears rose to her eyes. "I'm scared, Charles."

"Don't be." Charles pressed a tender kiss to her lips.

He pulled her closer, wrapping his arms around her naked torso. "We'll have a future. Together. We'll be free. Don't you want that?"

"I do."

"Then trust me."

She locked eyes with him, seeing her love for him reflected back at her. "I trust you."

He smiled at her. "Tell me you love me."

"I love you."

"Enough to spend eternity with me?"

"Eternity?" she asked, licking her lips. She knew what that meant.

"Yes, as a blood-bonded couple. Because the thought of you ever biting another person enrages me." As if to emphasize his statement, the lights in the room flickered, responding to the power inside him. "I want the only blood you ever drink to be mine."

"Charles..." Her gaze trailed to his neck, where a thick vein throbbed. She could hear the beating of his pulse, smell the richness of his blood. His witch's blood. Most vampires hated the taste of it, but not her. She loved it. Loved tasting him, drinking from him. Just as she loved the way he responded to her bite. She'd never seen a man turn so passionate and unrestrained. "My love." She ran her hand through his thick dark hair, pulling him closer. "As if I could drink another man's blood."

A flicker of excitement flashed in his eyes. He lifted his hand to her face, rubbing his thumb over her lower lip. "Show them to me."

Roxanne parted her lips and allowed her fangs to descend.

"God, you're beautiful," Charles whispered and pressed her back into the sheets, rolling over her.

She spread her legs automatically and felt his erection rub against her thigh. She loved that about him too—that he got hard so fast. It made her feel desired.

"I love you, Roxanne."

Gazing into her eyes, he plunged into her, his thick shaft filling her, stretching her. The first invasion was always like this: breathtaking, exhilarating, thrilling. And every time she craved it more. Craved *him* more. She'd never loved Silas like that. Not even before she'd discovered how evil he was.

But Charles... In him she'd found her soul mate. The only man who truly understood her and fulfilled her every need. Just like he did now.

His movements were slow at first, almost teasing. She wrapped her legs around his upper thighs, pulling him closer into her center.

Charles chuckled at her attempt to urge him to go faster and harder. "You little vixen. Think you can use your vampire strength to make me rush this?" He laughed. "Think again."

Before she knew what he was about to do, she felt a tightness around her wrists. Her eyes shot to them, but there was nothing to see. Nevertheless, invisible tendrils pulled her hands back, until they came to rest to either side of her head as if somebody was pinning her. Charles was using witchcraft to make her comply with his wishes.

"How devious," she murmured, though she couldn't suppress a smile, even though her hands were now tied by invisible ropes. Ropes not even her vampire strength could tear.

"Now be a good woman and let me make love to you the way you deserve it. Slowly and gently."

"Why do you think I deserve it?"

"Because you made me forget why witches hate vampires and see you for what you really are: a woman with a good and generous heart. And because I can't live without you."

She felt moisture collect in her eyes as she gazed at him.

"See," he whispered, tenderly stroking his fingers along her neck, down to her nipple, where he rubbed over the hard bud. "That's the woman I love. The woman who surrenders to me when I surrender to her."

Slowly he broke eye contact and lowered his head to her breast, capturing the peak and swiping his tongue over it. A strangled moan escaped from her throat and bounced against the walls of the hotel room.

"Then surrender already," she demanded.

"I am." He sucked harder, while he kneaded her flesh with his hand.

Farther below, his hips began to move, and he withdrew his cock before sliding back into her.

"I am surrendering," he repeated, plunging deeper and harder.

Suddenly she felt the restraints on her wrists loosening, and she didn't waste time and wrapped her arms around his shoulders, drawing him closer. The action made him thrust again. And again.

"Yes," she cried out and arched her back.

"Fuck, baby! You're gonna make me come too quickly."

"I don't care!" All she needed was to feel him shudder inside her to know everything would turn out alright. "Just love me."

"Always, my love, always."

She welcomed it when he started pounding into her, when he drove his cock deeper than she thought was possible. The sounds of their lovemaking were amplified in the small room of the dingy hotel. Moans and sighs bounced off the walls. But Roxanne could hear other sounds too, sounds Charles's witch hearing couldn't pick up: the sound of their heartbeats as they drummed more frantically, beating faster and louder with every second.

She felt the pleasure rise in her body, the waves of her approaching orgasm growing stronger, and she knew it was time.

Sliding her hand into his hair, she pulled him to her. His eyes sparkled in anticipation, and he tilted his head, offering her what they both wanted. That special connection that only a vampire's bite could create.

Underneath her palm, she felt him shiver.

"Oh, God, yes," he uttered with a groan, making her want him even more, because he gave himself so fully to her. Without restraints, without regret.

Her fangs itched, and she brought them to his skin. She licked over it, tasting the saltiness of his clean sweat, feeling the quivering vein beneath it. Unable to resist a second longer, she drove the sharp tips of her fangs into his neck and sucked on the plump vein.

Rich blood filled her mouth, while farther below, Charles's cock spasmed, and his seed poured into her. She swallowed her lover's blood, and as it ran down her throat, her entire body convulsed, her orgasm slamming into her like a tidal wave the size of a skyscraper. Together they rode the wave's crest, hovering suspended in an ocean of ecstasy.

Nothing had ever felt this right. This good. This perfect. Just like their future would be perfect.

She believed it then, in that moment. Believed it with all her heart. Her soul. Her life.

Only to have her trust in him obliterated two days later.

4

Today

After sleeping badly and dreaming even worse, Roxanne switched on her cell phone and sat up in bed. She had one message from the personnel department at Scanguards. They claimed that in order for them to release her last paycheck, Roxanne would have to come to the office for an exit interview. Yeah, she didn't believe that for a single second. Nevertheless, she got out of bed and headed for the shower, wondering why Gabriel was even bothering to try to get her to withdraw her resignation. It was a waste of time, if you asked her.

An hour later, she entered Mission HQ. She was ushered into Gabriel's office. But he wasn't alone. He'd brought in the big gun: Samson.

The owner of Scanguards, a handsome vampire with raven-black hair, hazel eyes, and a reputation for being fair and tough, pointed to a chair. "Take a seat, Roxanne."

She crossed her arms over her chest. "I'm not staying long."

Samson nodded, a contemplative look on his face. "Then let me make this short." He rose from his chair and came closer. "You're part of our family."

Where had she heard that before? Oh yeah, Silas. He'd always said things like that, though coming from Samson's mouth, the words lacked the menace that Silas had used to turn them into a threat.

"You've been with us for over twenty years, and we've all grown fond of you." He smiled. "The girls all look up to you."

"Vanessa wants to be like you," Gabriel threw in, referring to his seventeen-year-old daughter. "What am I gonna tell her if she finds out you're leaving us?"

Samson jerked his thumb over his shoulder toward Gabriel. "He's got a hard enough time keeping his kids in check. We'll have a riot on our hands, and they'll blame us for your leaving."

"You're exaggerating." It wasn't that she wasn't fond of the young hybrids, the half-vampire, half-human children of her bosses and colleagues, but there were more important issues at hand. She couldn't be in the same city as Charles. "They're young. They'll get over it."

"Will you?"

She clenched her jaw, knowing very well what he was alluding to. "I'm tougher than you think I am." She'd survived a devastating betrayal, she could survive this.

Gabriel rose from his chair and joined Samson. "And that's exactly why we need you. In fact, you're the only one who can help us with this case."

She glared at Gabriel. "I already told you I won't have anything to do with that devious witch. And neither should you! He's only going to screw you over."

"I'm afraid," Samson said calmly, "we have no choice. This is an assignment we can't afford to reject."

Roxanne scowled. "Don't you have enough money? How greedy—"

"It's not about money," Samson interrupted, his tone sharper now. "Far from it. We have reason to believe that Mr. Dubois is lying to us."

"His name isn't Dubois, it's Whedon. And I already told Gabriel that he's lying. What else is there to do but reject his request?" Didn't her bosses get that? They weren't normally this dense.

"The fact that he's lying, or rather, not telling us why exactly he needs heavy protection, is the reason we have to take this assignment," Samson explained, exchanging a look with Gabriel. "I spoke to Haven and Katie."

Roxanne shrugged, confused now. "What do Haven and Katie have to do with this?"

"Aside from Wes, they have the most experience with witches and their games. They share our suspicions."

Roxanne braced her hands on her hips, impatient. "Can you come to the point?"

"We believe there's something brewing in the witch world, and we want to make sure it doesn't boil over into ours. Call it caution. Call it a pre-emptive strike. But we need to find out what he's in town for."

Involuntarily Roxanne shook her head. "Oh no. No way. You're not using me to get dirt on that jerk and his witchy bullshit."

Samson took a step closer. "Please, Roxanne. I know you can do it."

"But I won't. I don't even want to be in the same town as that bastard, let alone in the same room. Protecting his worthless ass."

When Samson made a motion to speak again, Gabriel interjected, "Allow me." Then he looked at her. "After you left, Dubois, uh, I mean Whedon, said he believes you still love him and—"

"That fucking useless piece of—"

"—but what I got from that is that *he* still loves *you*. If anyone can get close to him, it's you."

That shut her up. She simply stared at Gabriel, unable to form a coherent sentence. Seconds passed, then she shook her head. No, Charles didn't love her. If he did, he wouldn't have betrayed her.

"Here's the plan: you'll be the lead on the assignment. We'll send you backup as soon as Quinn has changed the assignment roster and moved a few people around. In the meantime you'll go and scope things out, assess whether they need to be relocated to a more secure location."

"They?" she asked.

"Yes, he and his companion, a woman named Ilaria Dubois. She's the one he wants protected twenty-four-seven."

Roxanne's heart stopped. Charles had brought a woman? "Let me get this straight: you want me to protect Charles and his wife, and—"

"We don't know that she's his wife," Samson interrupted.

"Oh, please!" Roxanne hissed. "Why else would he want her protected? And on top of that you want me to get close to him so he'll tell me why he's really here?"

"That's it in a nutshell."

"And how am I supposed to do that when he's here with his fucking wife?"

Gabriel looked at her calmly. "As Samson said, she's probably not his wife. Or he would have said so. He called her his companion."

"I don't care what he calls her!" Because now she was furious. Charles had a woman, whereas she'd never been able to trust another man enough to have a relationship. And offers she'd had plenty, but nothing had ended up lasting longer than a night. And now Charles showed up in her town, completely over her, and apparently willing to go out of his way to rub her nose in it?

"Roxanne," Gabriel said softly, more softly than this intimidating man should be able to. "You're the only one who can get close to him. We need to know what he's planning. If you want to get back at him for whatever he did to you, this is your chance. You'll have our full support."

She looked into Gabriel's eyes and saw the sincerity in them. She shifted her gaze to Samson and saw the same expression in his.

"I'll do it under one condition."

"Name it," Samson said.

"If it turns out he's putting our world in danger with his actions, I want to be the one to kill him."

For a moment Samson was silent, contemplating her words. "If his actions warrant it... I'll make sure you'll be the one to dole out the punishment... whatever that may be."

She nodded. When it came to that, they'd finally be even, and she could lay her past to rest.

5

For the tenth time, Charles looked at his watch. He'd gotten the call from Scanguards headquarters almost an hour ago, advising him that they were taking the assignment and dispatching the bodyguards he'd requested for Ilaria immediately. About time, too. He'd almost given up on receiving a positive answer.

The corporate apartment he'd rented for their stay in San Francisco was on the top floor of a high rise near the waterfront and boasted a twenty-four-hour doorman. He'd called down to the front desk earlier to make sure the people from Scanguards were sent up right away.

When the knock sounded at the door, Charles pulled his shoulders back and took a deep breath, noticing that his ribs now felt completely normal, thanks to a healing spell and potion he had concocted after returning from his initial meeting at Scanguards. He had to hand it to Roxanne, she was no pushover. The only way to win her back would be with the truth.

Showtime.

Charles turned the door handle and pulled the door open. The sight of Roxanne took his breath away just as it had the previous night. For a moment, he drank in her features, then he pulled himself together and glanced down the hotel-like corridor.

"You're alone?"

She walked past him and entered the apartment. "My colleagues are on their way."

He let the door snap shut and watched her studying her surroundings.

"I don't like it," she said.

"The apartment?" he asked. It was generic, bare, and definitely on the cold side. He'd had worse. And he wasn't planning on staying here for long.

Roxanne looked over her shoulder, one side of her lip pulled up in a derisive gesture. "It's not secure."

"I chose it because it has a twenty-four-hour doorman."

She walked around the room, opening closet doors, looking out the window, and glancing at the hallway that led to the other rooms. "The front desk is a joke. I practically had to wake up grandpa down there. And there are multiple egress points that aren't sufficiently secure. The gate to the garage could easily be breached by anybody on foot, and somebody with a little bit of technical knowledge could override the keyed entry system in the elevators, bypassing the lobby altogether."

Her assessment felt sobering, and he tried not to take it personally. After all, he'd survived for nearly twenty-three years with various powerful witches hunting him. His preternatural senses had always warned him in time when anybody wanting him harm was near. They'd compensated for his lack of traditional security training. But the words nevertheless felt like a put-down. Coming from the woman he still loved as fiercely as when he'd left her, it stung like a hornet.

He tried to bite back a response, but couldn't. "Just as well that I didn't sign a long-term lease then."

A sound akin to a grunt came from Roxanne as she ambled into the open plan kitchen and examined the window over the sink.

"It can't be opened. Besides we're on the fourteenth floor. Bit difficult to climb up here, given the outside is glass," he said, still feeling he had to defend his choice of hiding place.

Roxanne shot him a displeased look. "I've got eyes." Then she marched out of the kitchen. "I think it's time I met Ilaria."

He was slow to reply. There were things he needed to tell Roxanne before the two met, because the hostility Roxanne exhibited toward him could ultimately endanger them all. "I wanted to explain a few things first. While it's just you and me."

She narrowed her eyes in suspicion. "Oh, I get it. You want to make sure that your wife doesn't find out about our—"

"My wife?"

She bobbed her head in the direction of the doors along the hallway. "Ilaria. No worries, I have no intention of airing our dirty laundry."

"Ilaria isn't my wife."

Roxanne shrugged, clearly not convinced. "Your girlfriend then. Or *companion*." She might as well have made air quotes around the last word. "I don't care what you fucking call her. Plaything maybe? Squeeze of the day?"

"He calls me his niece."

At the words, Roxanne whirled around and stared at Ilaria, who now stood in the corridor. She was dressed in jeans and a sweater, her lithe figure framed by long hair. Young and vulnerable, but not helpless. Her aura was shimmering in faint red tones, a sign that she was agitated.

"And I call him uncle," Ilaria added.

"I asked you to stay in your room until I called for you," Charles admonished, though he kept his voice calm and even, as he always did in her presence, particularly when anger was rising in her, wanting to burst to the surface. Only if he remained calm would he be able to help Ilaria find her equilibrium again.

"You taught me to defend myself. That's all I'm doing." She looked back at Roxanne and took a few steps toward her. "You must be Roxanne."

Roxanne nodded, but her reply was stiff. "Ilaria." When she turned and looked back at him, he saw confusion in her eyes. "You never told me you had a niece. Or siblings for that matter."

"I was about to."

She scoffed. "A little late for that."

"It's never too late for the truth," he contradicted her, searching her eyes, but she turned away, denying him the connection he wanted to establish.

"I need to check the rest of the place."

Ilaria pointed to the open door, still somewhat upset, though at least the color of her aura hadn't turned a darker shade. Somehow she was holding it together. "That's my bedroom. And this is Charles's. The bathroom is accessible from both bedrooms."

Roxanne walked to Charles's bedroom first, opened the door and walked inside. He knew what she'd find: a functional room without any decoration, the few things he possessed neatly hung in the too-large closet, his bed made.

He didn't follow her when she walked into the bathroom. Instead he walked to the open door of Ilaria's bedroom and waited until Roxanne entered the room through the connecting door. Surprise registered on her face, because Ilaria's room was nothing like his. It was decorated with loving care, with all the frills a young woman of twenty-three liked. Colorful and warm. Just like Ilaria herself.

"It's not real," he felt compelled to say.

Roxanne looked at him with a raised eyebrow.

"Everything you see is an illusion." He turned to Ilaria who'd sidled up to him. "Show Roxanne what the room really looks like.

"Do I have to? I like it like this."

"Just for a moment," he said, putting his hand on her forearm in reassurance. He was proud of her skills, though nobody except he ever got to see them.

Sighing, Ilaria made a sweeping gesture with her arm, and the room turned into the same bland and sterile environment as the rest of the apartment.

He could see that the display of witchcraft unnerved Roxanne, though she tried not to show it. Instead she looked at Ilaria, the question already leaving her lips. "Why do you do it?"

Ilaria shrugged and made another sweeping motion with her arm, turning the room back to its former state. "So it feels like home."

"Just don't get too comfortable," a cold male voice coming from the living room warned.

Shit! Ready for combat, Charles spun around, his arms raised to call the elements to help fight off the intruder, when he perceived the man's aura. Slowly he lowered his arms and squeezed Ilaria's arm to calm her, because she, too, had assumed a fighting stance, her aura turning darker.

"You must be from Scanguards," he said to the newcomer.

Behind the tall bald vampire, another man appeared. He looked a little younger, though one could never tell with vampires since they didn't age once they'd been turned. However, there was something different about the vampire with the dark hair and the youthful expression. His aura wasn't the same as the bald one's. In fact, he'd never seen such an aura before. Charles squinted. There was something human about him.

"My colleagues," Roxanne said from behind him, and Charles made space for her to exit the bedroom. She pointed to the bald vampire. "Zane." Then she motioned to the dark-haired man. "And that's Grayson."

As he and Ilaria followed Roxanne back into the living room, he noticed the displeased look on Zane's face, while Grayson's eyes seemed to be fixed on Ilaria. The young bodyguard ran his eyes over her, his lips parting in appreciation.

"So Gabriel sent you." Roxanne's voice interrupted Charles's observation.

Zane snorted. "For obvious reasons."

Charles sensed the open hatred in the vampire's demeanor. "Which are?"

"I hate witches."

Ilaria gasped, and instinctively grabbed Charles's arm for protection.

To Charles's surprise, Grayson stepped in front of Zane. "Don't mind him. It's nothing personal. He's always like that." He launched a charming smile at Ilaria. "I'll make sure nothing happens to you."

Charles felt like growling. This young pup really thought he could get into Ilaria's pants? His fatherly hackles rose at the thought, but at the same time he knew he was wrong to react this way. Even a father had to let go of his daughter one day, and after all, he was only her uncle. And Ilaria was old enough to make her own decisions now.

When Ilaria released his arm, Charles slanted her a look and noticed that under Grayson's admiring gaze her aura was suddenly glowing almost white. Pure. Good. Free of evil.

"You're not a vampire," Ilaria said, curiosity animating her voice.

"I'm a hybrid: half human, half vampire," Grayson replied. "My boss figured you might need somebody who can act unrestricted during daylight hours." He motioned to Zane and Roxanne. "Unlike pureblood vampires."

Charles nodded, appreciating the forethought. He'd heard of hybrids before, but had never encountered one. "And the fourth team member, when is he coming?"

"This is it," Zane stated.

"I requested four bodyguards."

Zane's jaw tightened. "I count as two."

"I should have guessed."

Zane narrowed his eyes. "Yeah, you should have." Then he exchanged a look with Roxanne. "We've gotta move them." He jerked his thumb over his shoulder, indicating the front door. "Piece of cake to open. And nobody heard us. Don't even get me started about sleeping beauty downstairs."

"We're on the same page," Roxanne replied. She turned to Charles and Ilaria. "Pack your stuff, and let's go."

6

While Ilaria and Charles packed their few belongings, Roxanne waited with Zane and Grayson. The few minutes she'd spent alone with Charles had already been more than she could handle. Why had she not stuck to her guns and told Gabriel and Samson that they could kiss her ass? But curiosity about Charles's companion had swayed her. As if she cared whether or not Charles was in a relationship with somebody. As it turned out, he wasn't. But she gained no satisfaction from that knowledge. Instead, it made her even more curious, when she should simply ignore him.

"We'll go in separate cars. It's safer that way. I'll take Ilaria," she now said to Zane. "You and Grayson take Charles. We'll meet at the safe house."

"Not a good idea," Zane replied. "Gabriel specified that the girl is our charge."

"I'm more than capable of protecting Ilaria by myself," Roxanne ground out between clenched teeth, not liking Zane's insinuation.

"I'm fully aware of that. But she's better off with me and Grayson. You handle her uncle."

She braced herself for an argument. "You might be more senior in rank, but I'm the lead on this assignment. I make the decisions."

"If I didn't know any better, I'd say you didn't want to be alone with Charles."

Anger churned up inside her. She poked her index finger into Zane's chest. "You keep your stupid remarks to yourself. I have no problems handling him." It was a lie, but she'd be damned if she allowed Zane to back her into a corner. "Go ahead. You and Grayson take Ilaria."

She pivoted to look at Grayson, glaring at him. "And you'd better keep your dick in your pants."

Grayson glowered back. "What the fuck? I'm not—"

"Aren't you?" She narrowed her eyes. "Let me give you a piece of advice. Never trust a witch. It'll only end badly."

Grayson opened his mouth to reply, but he didn't get the chance. Charles and Ilaria appeared, bags in hand. Shooting Roxanne a defiant look, Grayson sauntered toward Ilaria.

"Let me take your bag," he said, unleashing his devastating smile.

"You go first, we'll follow in my car in five minutes," Roxanne instructed, nodding at Zane.

Ilaria cast a questioning look at Charles.

"It's okay, Ilaria. Go with them. I won't be far behind," Charles reassured her.

When the door fell shut behind the three, Roxanne continued staring after them.

She heard him sigh. "Guess that means we have time to talk."

"We've got nothing to talk about."

"On the contrary."

She knew he was approaching her from behind even before she felt his hand on her shoulder. She tried to shake it off, but instead he gripped harder and turned her to face him.

"I can feel your hostility. Even your colleagues can sense it. It'll jeopardize this assignment."

Annoyance charged through her. "Are you questioning my professionalism?"

"Not for a second, but you deserve to know the truth about what happened that night. It will make things easier."

"I know what happened that night. You abandoned me. End of story." Even now, after twenty-three years, it still hurt as much as it had then. But she'd be damned if she'd admit this to Charles.

"I had no choice."

She scoffed. "Oh please, spare me your excuses. I'm over you."

"I make no excuses for what I did that night. But I want you to hear me out."

The pleading tone in his voice made her heart constrict painfully. But she had to remain strong and not fall for his lies again. Because that's all it would be: more lies to pacify her and to justify what he'd done. She turned back to the door and reached for the knob.

"The night you and I were supposed to leave, my sister Melissa brought Ilaria to me. Ilaria was three months old. Melissa was being chased by witches who had only one goal: to kill her infant daughter, my niece."

Roxanne hesitated at his words.

"Until that night, I didn't even know that my sister had given birth. We hadn't been in touch much. But she needed my help," he continued, his voice soft and calm. "Ilaria isn't just the daughter of a witch. She's special. She was born with the mark."

Roxanne turned to look at him, her forehead furrowing. He had her attention now. "What mark?"

"A birthmark that identifies her as a very special witch, one that will be more powerful and skilled than others. And therefore feared by those inferior to her. Witches of the mark have been hunted for centuries. There aren't many left, and those who are, live in hiding. When Melissa realized that Ilaria had the mark, she tried to hide it, but word got out, and she had to go on the run. She came to me that night and begged for my help. Begged me to protect Ilaria."

Charles ran a hand through his dark hair before continuing. "We were ambushed that night. Several witches had trailed Melissa to my house. We fought them off as best we could, but we knew we were losing the battle. When my sister handed me her daughter and begged me to protect her with my life, I knew what she was about to do. I couldn't say no."

Curiosity made her ask. "What did she do?"

"She went outside and fought against them with everything she had, giving me just enough time to escape out the back. She died that night protecting her child. And I'd made a promise to her. A promise I couldn't break. Ilaria needed me. She was helpless."

I needed you, too! Roxanne wanted to scream, but clamped her mouth shut.

"I went on the run with her. I never looked back. But I knew they'd never give up until they found her and killed her. I had to keep running."

"I could have helped you!" she ground out, pushing back the disappointment. He'd chosen a child over her. "We could have defeated the witches together."

Charles smiled a sad smile and shook his head. "No. I had to enlist help from other witches I trusted, and had I shown up there with a vampire in tow, they would have killed you before I'd even had a chance to explain. I did it to protect you."

"Bullshit!" she cried out. "You didn't want me anymore. And your niece was just a convenient excuse to rid yourself of me."

He didn't lose his cool. "That's not true, and you know it. Leaving you was the hardest thing I've ever done. I've regretted it a million times since."

Tears tried to push to the surface, but she forced them down. "Damn it! Damn you! You didn't even call me. You made no attempt to contact me. That's how much you loved me?"

"Yes, that's how much I loved you! Because had I contacted you, you would have been in danger, too. They would have tortured you to find out where I was. I couldn't let that happen. I couldn't let them hurt you, so I made sure nobody knew about you."

Roxanne swallowed back a rising sob, preventing it from bursting from her lips.

"I deleted all evidence about you from my cell phone before I tossed it for them to find. When I erased our call history, my heart broke, and when I deleted the last photo of you, I thought my life was over. But I had a responsibility, a duty I couldn't shirk."

Roxanne turned away, unable to listen any longer. "You could have at least sent me a message."

"You faked your death that night. I had no way of contacting you. And sending somebody with a note to our meeting place would have been too risky. Besides, if I had, you would have tried to find me." He sighed. "It was better that you hated me. At least then you wouldn't try to find me and land in the witches' crosshairs. You'd be safe."

"Safe?" she choked out. "Yeah, maybe from the witches. But Silas didn't buy my staged death. He came after me."

"Oh my God, baby, I'm so sorry."

He cupped her shoulders, turning her back to him, but she shook him off. His touch brought back too many memories and with it a yearning to turn back time.

"I don't need your pity. I killed him." And it had felt good to stake the sadistic son of a bitch. The world was better off without him.

"How?" Charles's one-word question was a mere echo.

"He'd sent his men away to deliver the appropriate punishment for my escape in private. He thought he could control me like he always did. But I had nothing to lose anymore. It gave me the strength I needed. I staked him, not expecting to succeed, thinking, hoping I would die instead. But I survived. Somehow. Silas was dead. I ran until I couldn't run any longer. His men never found me."

Charles nodded, his expression solemn. His gaze locked on her eyes, and his hand came up. "So strong, yet so vulnerable." He touched her jaw.

"Don't! You forfeited the right to touch me when you left me that night." She averted her eyes, turning her head to the side.

"Look at me, Roxanne, and tell me you hate me, and I'll never touch you again."

If that's all it took, she could do that. Slowly, collecting all her strength, she turned her head back to face his scrutinizing look.

"I hate you." Her voice cracked on the last syllable.

His fingers brushed over her cheek. "Say it again," he murmured, dipping his head toward her face, his gaze drifting to her lips.

"I hate you." But the words were even weaker than before.

"I never touched another woman after you."

Tears shot to her eyes. He wasn't playing fair. "No... no..."

"I only dream of you. Of holding you. Of loving you."

"I hate you." She repeated it like a mantra, but it didn't make it true. Yet it was all she could do to keep from breaking down.

"Maybe you do now, but if you gave us another chance..."

"It wouldn't change anything. I can't make twenty-three years undone."

"But you believe me, don't you?"

Did she? The story was fantastical, but so was their world. "It doesn't matter anymore whether I believe you." Two decades ago it would have mattered. But today it didn't make a difference. Too much pain had filled her heart. There was no place for love anymore.

"It matters to me. I need you to forgive me."

Roxanne swallowed. "There's nothing you can do or say..."

"There is something I can do," he murmured and sank his lips onto hers.

He took her completely by surprise. Maybe that was the reason she didn't immediately push him away and toss him across the room. Or maybe it was the way his lips pressed against hers, urging her to part them. Or the memories of their lovemaking that resurfaced with his sinful touch.

It could have been any number of things, but deep down she knew that she allowed it to happen because she wasn't done with him. She didn't hate Charles. But she couldn't trust him either.

7

The moment he felt Roxanne part her lips to take a breath, Charles dipped his tongue into her mouth. She tasted just as intoxicating as he remembered. As irresistible as she'd been back then. It was no wonder he was already hard. It was a wonder, in fact, that he'd been able to prevent his cock from bursting from his pants for as long as he had. Or that he hadn't stolen this kiss any earlier. Because he'd been craving it since the moment he'd discovered where she'd been all these years.

"Roxanne," he mumbled against her lips, releasing them for an instant only to grab hold of the seam of her top and shove it over her head. "I need you."

He captured her lips again, kissing her deep and hard, while he pressed her to him, his hands roaming her skin, searching and finding the clasp of her bra. When he snapped it open, she gasped into his mouth, and he swallowed down the sound with satisfaction.

Freeing her from the garment, he could finally touch her voluptuous breasts. He'd always loved kneading the responsive flesh, teasing her pert nipples, licking her silken skin. Not only because Roxanne represented everything a man could ever want, but also because of her reaction. Her moans and sighs were uncontrolled, and the way she pressed her body to his, asking for more, made hope bloom in his heart. She wasn't over him. Not by a long shot.

He ripped his lips from hers and dipped his head to her breasts, capturing one nipple in his mouth and sucking on it.

She breathed heavily. "This won't change anything between us."

If she wanted to lie to herself, so be it. But he knew better. It would change everything between them. He still had power over her, just as she did over him. To show her just that, Charles scraped his teeth along her skin and felt her shudder violently.

"You're still mine," he ground out and reached down to open the button of her pants. "And I'm still yours." He lowered the zipper and pushed down her pants.

Roxanne didn't stop him. Instead, she ripped his shirt open and pulled it off him. "Just because I'll let you fuck me, doesn't mean I'm gonna trust you again."

The words sounded bitter, but her actions were anything but. She opened his pants and shoved them halfway down his thighs.

"I'm not gonna fuck you, Roxanne." He gripped her hips with both hands and dragged her against his hard-on, letting her feel what she did to him. "I'm gonna make love to you."

"Oh no, you're not!"

She shoved him back until the back of his knees hit the couch. He lost his balance and fell backward. A moment later, she'd freed herself of her pants and sandals and was yanking his shoes and jeans off.

"We're gonna fuck," she said through clenched teeth and pulled off his boxer briefs, stripping him bare. "That's all you're gonna get."

"Fine. You wanna fuck? Let's fuck and see how long you can keep this up." He jumped up and grabbed her, lifting her off her feet and tossing her face down on the sofa. "That's what you want?"

"You have no idea what I want!"

He snatched her G-string and held it aside, not even bothering to free her from it. Instead he positioned himself between her legs and lifted her ass up. "I know exactly what you want."

He plunged inside her, seating himself balls-deep in her drenched pussy.

Fuck!

She was even tighter than he remembered. Or perhaps it only felt that way because he hadn't been with a woman since he'd left that night. He'd only known the comfort of his own hand in those dark, lonely nights. Dreaming of Roxanne. But no dream came close to reality. And this was reality. Roxanne beneath him, propped up on her elbows now, her hips rocking back to take him deeper.

He knew what she was doing: trying to prove that this was just sex. That it meant nothing to her other than some momentary physical pleasure, something any man could give her. But she was wrong if she thought she could fool him.

"Goddamn it, baby," he cursed and continued to thrust deep and hard. If he didn't slow down soon, he would come and lose this battle.

He slapped her hard on one cheek, knowing as a vampire she barely felt any pain, and pulled himself out of her.

"This isn't how this is gonna go down," he promised her and himself.

"I told you—"

He flipped her onto her back and yanked the G-string off her, before he spread her legs apart and sank his face onto her pussy.

Roxanne made a halfhearted attempt to pull away, but she didn't even use her vampire speed or strength against him, so he couldn't take her protest seriously. Instead, he lapped over her wet flesh and tasted her arousal, while he reached up with both hands to caress her breasts. Her protest died a silent death.

With every second he licked her, she turned back into the woman he knew. The woman who'd surrendered to him in bed, even though she was stronger than him. The woman who now writhed beneath his lips, undulating her hips for a deeper connection, for more friction. The woman who now angled her legs, placing one foot flat on the floor so she could lift herself closer to him.

"Yes," he murmured into her warmth and captured her clit between his lips, licking the swollen bundle of nerves harder and faster now. Just how she liked it. How she'd always liked it.

He could feel how close she was, and he wouldn't let her come alone. No, he would surrender to her, too. To show her that he trusted her.

Giving her clit another tug, he let go of it and sat up. Before she could protest at the interruption, he'd already positioned himself again and nudged his cock at her wet folds. Slowly, he edged forward, parting her nether lips with the tip and sliding into her. He noticed her lids flutter and the air rush from her lungs, while she arched her back off the cushions, thrusting her breasts and those hard nipples in his direction. Impossible to resist.

Only when his erection was fully submerged in her tight channel did he breathe again. A moan escaped him. This was what he'd dreamed of all those years. To feel her muscles tighten around him and imprison him.

He lowered himself over her and began to thrust, not wild and hard like he'd done before, but slowly and gently. Again, he captured one breast and licked her nipple, while kneading the other one. Roxanne followed his rhythm, or maybe he followed hers. It didn't matter.

She would be his again.

He lifted his head and captured her lips, kissing her passionately, until they were both breathless. But there was something else he needed.

Something only she could give him. He started to thrust faster, increasing his tempo to bring them both closer to their climax, before he released her lips and tilted his head to the side, offering his neck to her.

"Sink your fangs into me, Roxanne. Drink my blood."

Roxanne's body suddenly went rigid. A second later, he found himself on the floor halfway across the room.

She'd tossed him off her.

"How dare you?!" Fury spewed from her eyes. Her lips quivered, and hurt radiated from every pore of her body. "You have no right to demand this from me." She jumped up and collected her clothes, pulling them on faster than his eyes could follow. "You couldn't just fuck me, could you?"

Charles rose slowly. "I could never just fuck you, Roxanne. I always wanted more. I still do. And I won't give up until you've forgiven me, and are ready to sink your fangs into me again when we make love."

"Don't hold your breath."

8

Roxanne cursed silently as she opened the car door and slumped onto the driver's seat while Charles did the same on the passenger side.

Damn it! She'd nearly made the biggest mistake of her life: allowing Charles to get close again. Bad enough that she'd allowed him to touch her, that she'd *enjoyed* his touch, but to bite him again? Thank God she'd come to her senses at the last minute, because the intimacy of a bite during sex was more than she could handle. It would make her just as vulnerable as she'd been the night he'd left her. And it would make her heart ache just as much when he did it again. When he left her again.

"Roxanne, please…"

Instead of an answer, she rammed the gas pedal down, not waiting for Charles to put his seatbelt on.

She'd accepted his explanation of why he'd had to leave her, but that didn't mean she could forgive him. If he'd at least left her a message back then, she would have understood and not wallowed in self-doubt all these years, wondering why he'd left her. Why he'd deserted her the night she'd needed him most. It had shaken her trust in men to such an extent that she'd never been able to form relationships. She'd guarded her heart all these years, not wanting anybody to hurt what was left of it.

"You should have never come back," she spat, gripping the steering wheel tighter.

"I couldn't stay away any longer."

She shot him a sideways glance. "Oh, please don't tell me you came back because you finally found me."

He shook his head, then stared out the window. "I've known for a while now where you were."

That surprised her, but she didn't comment on it.

"It's how I found out about Scanguards. I was waiting for the right time to come. It wasn't supposed to be now. But things have started happening…" He sighed. "As fate would have it, Ilaria and I had to come to San Francisco. Ilaria's future is here. And by the looks of it, mine as well, though it will be separate from hers."

She tried to ignore his last words and instead asked, "What about her future?"

"It's time for her to be with her own kind."

"I thought you were her kind."

"I'm her *kin*, yes, but I'm not like her. She needs to be with witches who're like her, now that she's coming into her powers."

Immediately, Roxanne was reminded of how Ilaria had transformed her room with her powers. She'd seen witchcraft exercised quite often. Certainly Wesley, Scanguards' resident witch, was never shy about showing off his skills, but Ilaria's powers were something on a whole different level.

"I've guided her this far. My duty is nearly fulfilled. Soon..." He didn't finish his sentence.

There was something he wasn't telling her. She could sense it. Remembering the orders she'd received from Gabriel and Samson, she asked, "Why do you need protection for her now? She seems powerful enough to protect herself, if her little performance from earlier is anything to go by."

He blew out a breath through his nostrils. "Hmm. It's just a feeling. I want to make sure that nothing bad happens so close to the finish line."

"And the finish line is?" Because so far Charles hadn't given her any information that she could work with, nothing she could give to Gabriel other than the fact that Ilaria was born with *the mark*, whatever that meant.

"To unite Ilaria with her kind."

"Yeah, you said that. How exactly is that gonna happen?"

"I'm still working that out."

"This is not how Scanguards works. We need to know what's going on, and where we might encounter problems. Otherwise, how are we supposed to protect you?"

"I'm not the one who needs protection. Ilaria does. That's why I hired your team. I can take care of myself."

"Yeah, right!" she murmured under her breath.

His answer made her angry, but she tried to tamp it down. It was best not to show any emotions where Charles was concerned. He would only use them against her. Just like he had used her temporary vulnerability earlier to kiss her and coax her into sex.

Damn it!

She hadn't wanted to think of this again. Now she felt flushed, her heartbeat had accelerated, and moisture pooled at the juncture of her thighs. Her only consolation was that a witch didn't have the same sense of smell a vampire did, or Charles would realize that the mere memory of what had happened between them not half an hour earlier was still on her mind, and controlling her body's reactions.

"Trust me on this. Just protect Ilaria. Don't worry about me."

She scoffed.

"Not that you would, of course," he added. "Given the fact that you've tossed me across the room twice since I've returned. If I didn't know any better, I'd say you wanted to seriously hurt me."

She snapped her head in his direction. "Why don't you keep your smartass remarks to yourself?"

Unexpectedly, Charles smiled. "Because it seems to be the only thing that pushes you to communicate with me. And frankly, at the moment I'd even welcome you screaming at me if it means you'd acknowledge me."

She grunted to herself. She hated it when people pushed her buttons. And Charles was pushing them, all of them. She was glad that ten minutes later they arrived at the safe house. Roxanne drove the car into the garage and killed the engine. Without a word, she got out and marched toward the door leading into the two-story house. She didn't wait for Charles, though she was aware that he followed her with his travel bag in hand.

The hallway led to an open-plan living room and through to the kitchen. To her right was the front door and the stairs leading up to the second floor and to her left she saw doors to a laundry room and a guest bathroom.

Charles was just closing the door to the garage behind him when Zane came out of the living room, glaring at her. "You should have been here half an hour ago. What took you so long?"

She glowered back at him. "None of your fucking—"

"My fault," Charles interrupted. "I thought I sensed somebody following us, so I asked Roxanne to take a different route."

"Hmm," Zane grunted, then returned to the living room.

From the kitchen she heard noises. It sounded like Grayson was still trying to get into Ilaria's pants by turning on his charm. Men!

And while she was on the subject of men... She turned her head to look at Charles. "I don't need you to make excuses for me."

He raised an eyebrow. "Well, my bad. Why don't I get settled—" He motioned to his bag. "—and give you time to cool off."

"I don't need time to—"

But Charles was already marching upstairs. She whirled around and headed for the bathroom. The moment she'd locked the door behind her, she took a deep breath. Then another one. She would get through this. All she needed to do was to concentrate on her job.

She pulled her cell phone from her pocket and dialed Gabriel's direct line. He picked up almost immediately.

"Roxanne, what have you got for me?"

"Can you patch Haven in? I think he should hear this."

"Give me a sec."

She waited while Gabriel established the three-way call.

"It's Haven, what's up, Roxanne?" she heard her colleague ask a moment later.

"You know about the assignment I'm on, right?"

"Gabriel filled me in earlier. How can I help?"

"Do you have any way of contacting Wesley?" Never mind that she didn't particularly like him, but at least Wes might be able to help her figure something out.

"Sorry, I tried numerous times over the last few days, but it's going to voicemail. I can't even locate his cell on our GPS. Either the chip is broken, or..." He sighed heavily. "I have no idea where he is or how he's doing."

Hearing the worry in Haven's voice made her feel bad that she'd often treated Wesley with coldness. She knew Wesley didn't deserve it, but she hadn't been able to separate the man from the witch. "I hope he contacts you soon." She took a breath. "He has an extensive collection of books on witchcraft and history. Could you try and find something for me in those books?"

"What do you want me to look for?" came Haven's question.

"Charles told me that Ilaria, the witch we're supposed to protect, is his niece. Apparently she was born with *the mark*, whatever that means."

"What kind of mark?"

"I don't know. He didn't specify. But he said it makes her different from other witches. I need to know what that means. And why other witches would hunt her because of it."

"I'll do what I can," Haven promised.

"I appreciate it."

"Roxanne?" Gabriel now said.

"Yes?"

"Have you found out anything else? Why he's here? What he wants? Why he needs protection for her?"

Roxanne leaned back against the cool tile wall. "I'm working on it. But he's cagey. All he said was that Ilaria needs to be with her own kind. And that her future is here in San Francisco."

"Have you tried to get close to him to make him trust you again?" Gabriel probed.

Yeah, and look how that turned out! She wanted to scream, but clamped her jaw shut. It had landed her underneath Charles, panting and moaning, begging for release. Vulnerable. Weak.

Shit!

"Roxanne?" Gabriel asked again.

"I'm working on it. Gotta go."

Roxanne disconnected the call before Gabriel could say anything else. She should have never let herself be talked into taking this assignment. Now she was caught between—well, between what and what? Her heart and her head? Her past and her present? Her duty and her desires? Whatever it was, she was trapped. And the door to the trap she found herself in was slowly closing.

If she were smart, she'd make a run for it and get away while she still could.

9

Even after a long shower, during which he'd had to satisfy himself just to get any semblance of brain function back, his desire for Roxanne was as strong as before. By asking her to bite him, he'd gone too far, too fast. If only he could have reined in his need for this intimacy a little longer, then maybe he would be a step further in his bid to win Roxanne back. But no, he'd had to push his luck. Twenty-three years without her had made him impatient.

After reassuring himself that Ilaria was taken care of, Charles withdrew to one of the bedrooms on the second floor, telling Roxanne and her team that he was going to sleep. Nobody questioned him. After all, witches weren't nocturnal like vampires. But he didn't sleep. Instead, he took a map from his travel bag and spread it on the floor in front of the bed. From a side pocket he retrieved a crystal on a leather string.

He reached for the tissue on the bedside table. A blotch of red, dry by now, was in its center. Blood from Ilaria, not just from any spot on her body, but taken from her mark. She'd agreed to it without protest, knowing what was at stake. He wrapped the blood-stained tissue around the crystal.

Cross-legged he sat down, stretched his hand holding the string out over the center of the map and closed his eyes. He hummed a soft melody, while concentrating on his solar plexus. As warmth spread from cell to cell, he felt a tingling in his arm traveling down to his fingers. He allowed it to release into the string and reach the crystal. It began to swing.

He'd done this several times before they'd come to San Francisco, starting when Ilaria had first come into her powers. And now that she was getting stronger, the readings he got became more accurate. It was time to make contact, though he was sure they already knew that Ilaria was here. Just like Charles could sense his niece's power, so could other witches. And that fact made his quest more urgent with every day that passed. Soon, more and more witches would hunt them, and there would be no place to run anymore. No place to hide what she was.

When the crystal dropped to a spot on the map, drawn to it like metal to a magnet, he bent over the map. Golden Gate Park.

Charles rose and packed away his tools, slipped on his jacket, and listened for sounds from downstairs. It was quiet, but he knew the vampires were awake. Earlier, he'd heard Zane leaving the house to do a perimeter check. He was back now, pacing the downstairs hallway. No human would be able to leave the house without him knowing, for a vampire's hearing was so sensitive, it would pick up any sound.

Luckily, Charles wasn't human, and while he didn't move as stealthily as a vampire, he had other skills. A silencing spell made sure no sound left his bedroom while he slid open the window and peered outside. The house was built on a steep hill, and though he was on the second floor, the drop on this side of the house was less than ten feet. Charles hoisted himself through the window, lowered himself, then let go of the window sill and dropped down into the overgrown garden. For a moment he remained frozen, listening intently, but nothing moved inside the house.

It didn't take long to reach the main road. He looked around. No sign of a taxi or other transportation. It didn't matter. From what he'd gathered from the map, he was less than three miles away from the spot in Golden Gate Park that the crystal had pointed to. Charles fell into an easy jog.

He reached a clearing surrounded by mature trees and high bushes. Moonlight filtered through the trees, casting shadows onto the ground. Charles stopped in the middle of the meadow and waited. He could feel the collective power that surrounded him. It was different from the power he felt from other witches. Stronger, more potent.

All of a sudden, the shadows began to move, separating themselves from the trees. Remaining still, he watched them approach. Three of them, more shadow than form, more ghost than living being. The witches of the mark. Their aura identified them as different from other witches. It drew him to them like moth to a flame, a sign of their banked power surpassing his. The air crackled with electricity. Tension rose like mist.

"You found us," an ethereal sounding voice said, "yet, you are not one of our kind."

He nodded. "I need your help."

One of the shadows moved closer. "It is not you who needs our help," a second voice claimed. "We can sense one of our own near."

"My niece, Ilaria. She's one of you."

"How old is the child?"

"She's no child anymore. She's twenty-three."

A gasp went through the three shadows. "And she's still alive?" One figure came closer and finally he could see her. A woman of indistinguishable age, neither beautiful nor ugly. She gave him a once over. "And you have protected her for all this time?" She mumbled something to herself. "Despite the danger to yourself? Why?"

"She's my flesh and blood."

"Even fathers and mothers have killed their children once they recognized the mark, knowing what the future holds. Knowing the dangers."

"I made a promise."

She nodded. "How much longer does she have?"

"Not long. With every day, the evil comes closer."

"Did you bring what we need?"

He reached into his pocket and produced a photograph. He'd taken it only days ago, printing it at a twenty-four hour self-service printing shop before coming to San Francisco. A picture of Ilaria's mark.

It was pulled from his fingers and lifted into the air, only to land in the witch's hand a moment later. The witch studied it, before lifting her head, surprise flickering brightly in her eyes.

"I'm surprised she hasn't killed you yet."

He knew that. He also knew he wouldn't be able to dodge that bullet for much longer. "Will you save her?"

"Does she want to be saved?"

10

Roxanne rose and retrieved a gun from a hidden panel in the living room of the safe house. She didn't often use a gun, but on certain assignments she liked to be armed to the teeth.

"Perimeter check?" Zane asked.

She nodded. "See you in five."

"Want me to come with you?" Grayson called to her, popping his head through the open doorway leading to the kitchen.

"I can handle a fucking perimeter check," she growled and marched to the door.

"Gee, I was just asking."

She knew why she'd snapped at the young hybrid. She was still annoyed with herself about how she'd handled Charles. His words continued to echo in her mind. *I won't give up until you've forgiven me.* But how could she forgive him when his actions had caused her years of pain? How could she put that behind her?

Snatching her parka off the hook near the entrance, Roxanne opened the door and stalked outside. Her training kicked in, and she studied her surroundings. The lot the house sat on backed up to a grassy slope that ended in a dense patch of woods on one side of a hill. The front looked out over the houses farther below. It was a good vantage point. Any car coming up the narrow street could be seen from afar.

Roxanne rounded the corner to the tiny back yard, pulling the parka tighter around her torso, though she didn't really feel the cold night air, not like a human would. Or a witch. Involuntarily, she lifted her eyes up to the second floor where Charles slept. Through the open window, she saw light in Charles's room. Maybe he wasn't sleeping after all. Maybe he was just avoiding her? And if he was, could she really blame him? After all, she'd treated him with open hostility even after he'd told her why he'd had to leave her. Any reasonable person would have accepted his explanation. Any reasonable person would have forgiven him by now. But she couldn't shake the suspicion that he hadn't told her everything. His refusal to elaborate on why he'd come back now and what he was planning made her uneasy.

She let her gaze roam toward the woods, but all was quiet there. Then she looked back at the window when it struck her. Why was his window open? It was a cool night, and the house wasn't particularly warm in the first place. Her skin prickling with awareness, she turned on her heel and marched back to the entrance.

When she walked inside, she hung her parka back on the hook and looked up the stairs. Was she just looking for an excuse to talk to Charles, or was she truly concerned about the open window? No matter the reason, she set one foot on the first step.

"Going upstairs?"

She snapped her head to the side. Zane had startled her. "Do you have to sneak around like that?"

"I don't have to." He managed a half-smile, though barely. "But I like to."

"Sick, just sick," she ground out and walked upstairs. "I'm checking on them."

"Need help?"

"No."

"You know what you're doing, I suppose," Zane said with a smugness in his tone that made her want to smack him.

Yes, it was her fucking business if she wanted to talk to Charles. But did she really know what she was doing? By going to him now under pretense, wasn't she putting herself in the same situation again? Wouldn't he see right through her like he always had? Would he see the woman who wanted a second chance, but didn't have the faintest idea how to go about it, how to leave her past behind and start fresh?

At the door to Charles's bedroom, she hesitated. Inside her a battle raged.

Don't let him hurt you again, one voice said. *Give him another chance*, another argued.

Before she could decide which voice had more weight, she was already knocking at the door. There was no reply. But she'd come this far. She couldn't turn around now.

She turned the knob and opened the door. "Charles…"

Her words died when she saw the empty, unused bed. She glanced around the room. Charles was gone.

"Shit!"

She rushed out of the room and ran to the bedroom Ilaria occupied. Without knocking she swung the door open. The light from the hallway fell onto the bed, illuminating the young witch. Roxanne rocked to a halt. What she saw was impossible!

Ilaria was lying face down, the covers down at her knees, wearing pajama bottoms and a cotton bra that exposed most of her back. She was hovering several inches off the bed!

But that wasn't the worst of it. After all, she was a witch, and some witches had impressive powers. But what Roxanne saw on Ilaria's back was much more frightening. She slammed her hand over her mouth to prevent herself from screaming.

But Ilaria had heard her nevertheless. She suddenly dropped back on the bed, whirled around and shot up, reaching for the sheet to cover her front.

"The mark," Roxanne murmured, unable to believe what she'd seen with her own eyes.

With the frightened eyes of a doe Ilaria stared at her, scrambling back, pulling her knees up to her chest as if to protect herself.

But Roxanne had already seen what Ilaria was trying to hide. Intricate signs and symbols criss-crossed Ilaria's back. The design took up nearly half her upper back. Roxanne would have dismissed it as a tattoo had she not seen the symbols pulse like the heartbeat of a living being. Whatever was embedded in Ilaria's back was alive. Alive and dangerous.

"Don't hurt me!" Ilaria begged in a voice so faint Roxanne didn't even know whether she'd heard her speak it or whether she'd simply interpreted the frightened girl's expression.

The sound of footsteps on the stairs announced the approach of her colleagues. Roxanne flipped the light switch, bathing the bedroom in warm light just as both Zane and Grayson barreled upstairs and appeared behind her.

"What's wrong?" Zane asked, the tone in his voice indicating that he was on high alert.

"Charles is gone."

"Fuck!" Zane cursed.

"How the fuck did he get past us?" Grayson asked. "I heard nothing."

But Roxanne knew better what Charles was capable of. She should have been prepared. "Probably used a spell to leave the house unnoticed." She glared at Ilaria. "Where did he go?"

Ilaria's lips quivered, her eyes shifting to Roxanne's hand. Roxanne followed her gaze and realized only now that she'd drawn her weapon and was holding it in her hand. No wonder Ilaria was scared. Slowly Roxanne holstered the gun, but before she could repeat her question, her cell phone rang. She pulled it from her pocket and checked caller ID.

"Haven," she said to her colleagues and answered the call. "What have you got for me?"

"You're not gonna like it," the witch-turned-vampire started.

"Let me make that decision."

"Well, I found a lot of stuff about marks and such. But most of it was inconsequential, except for one particular mark. It's called the *Mark of Cain*. Any witch born with the *Mark of Cain* is considered property of the devil, born evil. It says once she attains all her powers, she'll be able to destroy mankind."

"Fuck!"

"You said it," Haven replied. "Witches carrying the mark are hunted by every coven. They're feared because of their power, because they use it for evil, so the good witches of this world formed a group of slayers with the sole mission of killing witches with the mark."

"Is there anything about what this mark looks like?" Roxanne asked, though she already knew the answer.

"I'll read it to you: the mark manifests as a birthmark in the form of a pentagram, growing with each year into an intricate design of symbols—"

"—and signs that pulse as if alive," Roxanne finished.

"How the—"

"I've just seen one."

"Ah shit! You gotta get out of there, now!" Haven yelled through the phone. "When it pulses, the evil wants to break through. You can't stop it. Once the evil is unleashed, nobody can defeat it."

"Thanks, Haven, I'll keep that in mind."

"Roxanne, you've gotta—"

Roxanne disconnected the call and shoved the phone back in her pocket. A sideways glance told her that her colleagues had heard every word Haven had spoken.

Their guns were pointed at Ilaria. The girl shrieked.

"I'm not evil," Ilaria whimpered. "Please, I'm not evil. I'm fighting it. Charles, he helps me fight it." Tears sprang from her eyes.

Roxanne had never seen a person so scared. When she locked eyes with Ilaria, suddenly her own past washed away, and all she saw was a child that needed protection, a child that would have been killed had it not been for the man who put his own desires aside to protect her.

"I won't hurt you," Roxanne murmured and approached slowly so as not to frighten the girl even more.

"Stay back, Roxanne," Zane warned. "It's not safe."

She looked over her shoulder and motioned him to remain calm. "She's just a girl." Then she continued her approach.

Ilaria watched her every step, shivering uncontrollably. "Don't." She lifted her hand. "Please. Don't come any closer. What if *it* tries to hurt you?"

"You won't let it," Roxanne coaxed softly. "You're stronger than that." At least she hoped so. Ilaria had to be stronger than the evil that was trying to control her. Or they would all perish.

Roxanne swallowed her fear and sat down on the bed, then gently pulled Ilaria into her arms. For a few seconds, Ilaria remained stiff, but then, hesitantly, she slid her arms around Roxanne's back and held on for dear life. Roxanne brushed her hand over the girl's hair, when the sound of the front door slamming startled her.

Ilaria screamed. Beneath her other hand, Roxanne felt the mark pulse anew.

"Help me," Ilaria cried out.

11

Charles raced up the stairs, panic giving him wings. He'd heard Ilaria's cry and sensed her fear. Something had happened, and he hoped he wasn't too late.

The moment he reached the second floor landing, Zane blocked his path, a gun pointed at him.

"What the fuck?" Charles cursed.

"Where've you been?" Zane pressed out through a clenched jaw, his eyes glaring red.

"What have you done to Ilaria?"

He shoved the bald vampire out of his way, knocking him against the wall with a short burst of his power, and charged through the open door into Ilaria's room. He skidded to a halt. The scene playing out inside Ilaria's room wasn't at all what he'd expected.

Though Grayson was armed like Zane had been, his weapon was lowered, and he was silently staring at the two women on the bed: Roxanne was holding a crying Ilaria in her arms, comforting her, caressing her exposed back, calming the pulsing mark. His mouth dropped open as he saw how the mark began to pulse more slowly, its evil weakening under Roxanne's gentle touch. Slowly, in front of his eyes, Ilaria's red aura turned purple, then blue, until it got lighter and lighter.

Having heard or sensed his arrival, Roxanne's head turned to him, her eyes full of empathy and understanding.

"Your uncle is here," she murmured to Ilaria and made a sign for him to approach.

His feet carried him to the bed, and slowly, gently, Roxanne eased herself out of Ilaria's embrace and transferred the girl to him.

"I was so scared," Ilaria whispered at his neck.

He stroked his hand over her hair. "I'm here now, honey, I'm here. Everything will be alright."

She lifted her head, a ray of hope shining in her eyes. "Did you find them?"

He nodded.

A shiver went through her, and her voice trembled, as she asked a second question, "Will they help me?"

He smiled and kissed her on the forehead. "They will come for you tomorrow night."

All the tension left her lithe body, and she sagged against him.

"Rest now. I'll be close by."

She nodded and allowed him to tuck her in, before rising from the bed and turning back to Roxanne. Roxanne and Grayson had retreated to the door, and Zane was now standing behind them, glaring in open hostility. When nobody moved, he motioned to the hallway behind them.

"Downstairs," Charles said.

"Somebody has to watch her," Zane grunted, making a gesture with his gun hand.

"No," Charles insisted. If Ilaria sensed a threat against her—and it was hard not to see Zane as a threat—the evil in her would rise again, trying to protect itself. "She'll be fine."

Still Zane didn't stand down. To Charles's surprise, Roxanne suddenly said, "Let it go, Zane. We'll discuss it downstairs."

Narrowing his eyes, Zane growled, but then pivoted and marched toward the stairs.

Charles exchanged a look with Roxanne. He could see the many questions in her eyes. And finally, he would answer them all.

Moments later, he was facing Zane, Grayson, and Roxanne in the living room.

"You should have told me," Roxanne began.

Charles blew out a breath through his nostrils and shoved a hand through his hair. "Scanguards would have never helped me if I'd told you how dangerous the situation is."

"You mean how dangerous Ilaria is," Zane interrupted, a hostile tone in his cutting voice.

Charles glowered at him. "It's not Ilaria who's dangerous. It's the mark. The evil inside her."

But Zane wasn't satisfied. "Same thing!"

Roxanne lifted her hand to stop her colleague. "Let him explain."

Charles nodded, grateful that Roxanne wasn't condemning him outright. After all, she had every reason to do so: he'd kept a vital piece of information from her, lied to her in fact, though he'd hated doing it. But the time for lies was past now.

"The mark Ilaria carries on her back is something every witch fears. Generations of witches have tried to eradicate it, because it spreads pure evil in this world and it turns its host into a willing participant once he or she has given up resistance. The way to stamp out this evil has always been to kill the witch who carries it. It's our duty to do so. So that all of us and all of you will be safe." He looked straight at Zane, then at Roxanne. "I know that Scanguards has collaborated with witches before. Had I told you about the true meaning of Ilaria's mark, any witch in your acquaintance would have advised you to kill Ilaria immediately."

"Seeing how the mark pulses, I wouldn't have needed somebody to tell me to shoot it," Zane growled.

Charles nodded. "The first time it started pulsing, I was afraid, too. But fear only makes it worse. It gives it power." He looked at Roxanne, his heart warming at the recollection of how she'd comforted his niece. "You weren't afraid. It helped Ilaria fight it. I thank you for that."

"Haven warned me," Roxanne said.

"Haven?"

"A colleague. I had him do some research for me. He found writings about the mark. He called just as I realized you were gone. I went into Ilaria's room, looking for you and found her sleeping, but the mark wasn't."

Charles's heart stopped. "It was active while she slept?"

When Roxanne nodded, her brows furrowed, he swallowed hard.

"What does that mean?" she asked, clearly anxious because he hadn't said anything for several seconds.

"You'd all better sit down." All three bodyguards remained standing, and all three suddenly seemed to widen their stances as if preparing for battle. Their instincts were solid, and he hoped they'd be on his side once the inevitable battle ensued. Shrugging, Charles corrected, "Well, I guess standing works, too."

Charles looked at the ceiling, listening, but upstairs everything was quiet. Then he lowered his gaze and looked at the three vampires. "One in a thousand witches is born with the mark. It looks like a perfect tattoo at first. A tiny pentagram. It has no power when it's that small. But as it grows, it matures, developing more symbols, more signs. Getting stronger. And it starts influencing the child, exerting control over it. The child becomes difficult to handle. It lashes out at its parents, its siblings, anybody the mark perceives as a threat." He sighed deeply. "When

Ilaria was put in my arms as a three-month-old, I knew it would be difficult to keep her on the right path and give her the strength to reject evil. But I never knew how much it would cost me."

He looked at Roxanne, searching her eyes, trying to make her understand. It had cost him Roxanne's love.

"I knew the reasonable thing would have been to kill my niece, so she would never have to suffer, and never hurt anybody."

"It was fucking selfish of you to let her live!" Zane growled.

"Selfish? You can call it what you want. But I made a promise to her mother. I was torn, and in those moments when I wavered, Ilaria gave me the greatest gift: the love of a child for her parent." He felt tears rise to his eyes and turned away, pretending interest in the old fireplace. "I knew then that I could never kill her. I hid what she was as best I could. We never stayed anywhere for long. And all the while I searched for the other witches of the mark."

"There are more like her?" Roxanne echoed.

He was slow to answer. "Yes. The same, yet different. They've conquered the evil, and now *they* control the mark on their body. *It* doesn't control them." He turned to face Roxanne and her colleagues again. "Don't get me wrong, they're still powerful witches, more so than I or any other witch I know. When they're present, you can feel their power. It draws you to them, puts you at their mercy. But they don't hurt people, not unless they feel threatened. They're not controlled by evil any longer."

"How?" Roxanne asked.

"I don't know. Maybe it's their combined willpower, maybe a secret ritual. Nobody knows. It's their secret, one they'll only share with their own kind. I only know that I have to deliver Ilaria into their care. It's her only salvation. And ours." He sought Roxanne's eyes. "I lied to you when I said that the witches that were hiding us would have killed you, because you're a vampire, had I taken you with me. That's only partially true."

"What?" Grayson croaked, tossing a confused look between Charles and Roxanne as if playing ping-pong. "You know each other from before?"

"Oh, please, keep up," Zane grunted. "Anybody could see that, but clearly you only have eyes for the girl."

"Jerk!" Grayson hissed at Zane.

"How Roxanne and I know each other is a story for another day," Charles said, addressing Grayson, before looking back at Roxanne. "I didn't know if I could control the evil in Ilaria. Had I taken you with me on the run, Ilaria could have killed you during one of her fits." And he would have never been able to forgive himself for that.

"Fits?" Grayson now said.

"Moments when the mark is trying to exert power over her. She lashes out at everybody in those moments, gets violent. The more fear and hatred people around her exhibit during one of those episodes, the stronger the mark reacts." He smiled at Roxanne. "By trusting her not to hurt you, you helped her fight against it. I saw her aura change right before my own eyes—from a volatile red to a calm blue."

"I couldn't see the changing colors in her aura," Roxanne said.

"Only witches can see that kind of depth in their fellow witches' auras. Other preternatural creatures can only identify that her aura is that of a witch. I saw her colors change when you comforted her. You made the evil subside. For now. But not for much longer."

Roxanne breathed heavily, clearly affected by his words. "What are we gonna do?"

"Get backup before Ilaria kills somebody," Zane snapped.

Roxanne whirled around to him. "Didn't you hear what Charles just said? If we show fear and hatred, the evil will lash out."

"Well, what do you suggest? Hug her to keep her and us safe?" Zane snorted in disgust.

"While that's a little too simplistic, it does help temporarily," Charles had to admit.

Zane glared at him and gritted, "I was joking."

"Could've fooled me." Charles doubted that the vampire was capable of a joke. Or a smile. A tender embrace would really stretch the imagination.

"Charles, focus," Roxanne demanded. "What can be done?"

"I've already done it."

"Done what?" Zane asked full of suspicion.

"Tonight I sought out the witches who conquered their marks. They're willing to take her and help her fight the evil. Tomorrow night."

"Oh crap," Zane cursed. "More fucking witches."

"I don't know what you've got against witches," Grayson threw in, crossing his arms over his chest. "I like them."

"You just want to get into his niece's pants," Zane snarled.

Anger made the hybrid's eyes glare red. "Don't be so disrespectful. Her uncle is standing right here."

But Zane wasn't bothered by such a tiny detail. "I'm not fucking blind, am I?"

"Stop it!" Roxanne yelled. "Both of you! We have a decision to make."

"I've made mine," Zane claimed.

She glared at him. "As a team." Then she looked at Charles, and her expression softened. "Will you be able to control her until tomorrow night?"

Barely. Now that the evil was manifesting while she slept, it wouldn't be long until Ilaria would lose her valiant fight. "I'll need help."

"Anything I can do," Roxanne offered.

"Not from you." He motioned to Grayson. "From him."

Grayson pointed to his chest, which seemed to swell a little. "From me?" He grinned. "What do you want me to do?"

"How are you with compliments?"

Grayson grimaced. "What the...?"

"When Ilaria wakes, I want you to distract her. Pay her compliments, flirt with her. Keep her occupied. Make her think you're interested in her, like a young man would be interested in a young woman. Tell her she's pretty."

"Sure, but why?" Grayson asked, clearly confused, yet definitely interested.

"Because love helps her fight evil. When Ilaria first set eyes on you, her aura changed to the purest white I've ever seen. It signified goodness and purity. Somehow when she's with you, she's stronger, so much stronger than I've ever seen her. If she believes a handsome young man is interested in her, it'll help her more than I could at this point. It might just be enough to see us through the next twenty-four hours until the witches come to take her."

"Of course, I can do that. No problem." The words sputtered from Grayson's mouth, but Charles didn't miss the grin that was spreading on his lips.

"That's just sick," Zane grunted to himself.

Charles ignored him, and addressed Grayson instead. "Oh, and Grayson, that's not a license to get into her pants. Do you understand me?"

"Sure."

Charles had to turn away from the hybrid's smirking face, or he was likely going to smack him. But right now, he didn't think he had any other choice. Ilaria was too close to the edge. A wrong word could tip the balance of power between her and the evil inside her. A young tomcat like Grayson might be just the right medicine for now.

"I still say we get backup," Zane insisted now.

"I thought you said you counted for two," Charles replied, not liking the vampire's combative attitude.

"Nice try, buddy, but insulting me won't change my decision. Roxanne, I'm going to call HQ, whether you like it or not. This is a job for more than three people. Particularly since Romeo here"—he motioned to Grayson—"won't be any use at all should something go wrong."

She nodded. "Fine. Get backup, but don't have them come to the house. I don't want Ilaria to feel threatened. Have them stationed around the perimeter."

Zane pulled his phone from his pocket and marched into the kitchen.

"Grayson, why don't you give us a moment," Roxanne said.

"Why... uh... oh. Sure, yeah. I'll just... wash my hands, or something." He awkwardly sauntered out into the hallway and disappeared into the bathroom.

Suddenly alone with Roxanne, there was silence. Charles shifted his weight from one foot to the other. He had come clean. No more secrets. No more lies. Now he needed to find out where they stood.

Yet he hesitated. He'd said everything there was to say. There was nothing else to reveal. He'd told her already that he loved her. That he'd never touched another woman after her. That he still wanted her.

The ball was in her court. It was up to her now to take the next step.

Roxanne made a motion as if readying herself for something difficult. His heart leapt, filling with hope.

But whatever Roxanne had wanted to say or do, didn't happen.

Because the earth beneath their feet began to shake.

12

The earthquake couldn't have been more than a 5.5 on the Richter scale. Nevertheless Roxanne's heart began to beat rapidly, while she braced herself as the familiar rolling waves tried to rob her of her balance.

Within ten seconds, it was all over. She did a quick assessment of everything around her. A painting on the wall hung askew, but it hadn't fallen down. A vase had tipped over, but fallen, safely, on a cushion.

Roxanne sighed with relief and gave Charles, who looked a little bit shaken, a reassuring smile. "Probably only a five pointer."

"More like a five point three," came Grayson's reply from the hallway as he strolled into the living room.

The door behind Roxanne opened.

"Barely a four point eight," Zane claimed coming out of the kitchen.

"You're not even a native Californian," Grayson said. "What do you know about earthquakes?"

Roxanne rolled her eyes. Those two got increasingly competitive the more time they spent with each other.

"More than you, considering I've lived in this state longer than you have." Zane pulled his phone from his pocket and waved it in Grayson's direction. "Wanna bet I'm right?"

But instead of answering, Grayson turned his head to the hallway. "The earthquake woke Ilaria."

Roxanne listened. Grayson was right.

"I'll check on her," Charles said and rushed past her, waving to Grayson. "You're coming with me. I doubt she'll want to sleep now. There are likely to be aftershocks. Somebody should keep her company."

Grayson grinned and followed Charles upstairs. Roxanne watched both of them disappear and heard them enter Ilaria's room.

"Damn earthquakes," Roxanne muttered and turned back to Zane, who was making a phone call on his cell.

"Hey baby girl," he said in hushed tones, tones that were much softer and gentler than he used with his colleagues. Only when he spoke to his wife did Zane sound friendly. Clearly, Portia, his blood-bonded mate, knew how to bring Zane out of his hard shell.

"How are you and the boys? Did anybody get hurt?"

Roxanne busied herself adjusting the painting on the wall, not wanting to listen in on Zane's conversation.

"About the earthquake of course," Zane said, his voice a little louder now.

Something in it made her look at him and notice the deep frown lines that now appeared on his forehead. Their gazes collided. Something was wrong.

"So you didn't feel it then?" Zane hummed, listening to her response. "No, no, it wasn't strong. Maybe just a three pointer." Alarm flared in his eyes as the lie rolled over his lips. "Didn't mean to alarm you. No, everything's fine. Hug the boys from me, okay? Love you, baby girl." He disconnected the call.

"It's impossible that Portia wouldn't have felt it," Roxanne said.

"Exactly my thinking." He tapped on his iPhone. "We're on bedrock here, my house isn't. If we felt it, my house would have shaken even worse."

Roxanne approached so she could see the screen of his cell phone. "What's the CGS say? Any alerts yet?"

Zane shook his head. "None."

Roxanne pulled out her own phone and opened a social media site. "Social media is faster than the California Geological Survey. I bet you a hundred teenagers have already posted or tweeted about it, or whatever they do." She scrolled through a multitude of posts. Not a single one mentioned an earthquake in Northern California.

"I'm calling HQ," Zane said, urgency evident in his tight tone.

She was nodding when she heard sounds on the stairs. Charles's long legs entered her line of sight and she walked toward him as he came down the stairs, meeting him under the door frame.

"Is she okay?"

He nodded. "Just a little agitated. But Grayson is telling her stories about his siblings and how they made a game of guessing the strength of an earthquake on the Richter scale." He smiled. "It seems to distract her."

"Good. Because something isn't right."

"What?" Alarm colored Charles's voice.

She motioned him into the living room, away from the hallway where their voices might carry upstairs.

"We can't find any evidence of an earthquake," she explained.

His eyes narrowed. "Come again? I felt the earth shake underneath my feet."

"Fuck!" Zane cursed, making Roxanne and Charles whirl their heads toward him. "There was no earthquake. Nowhere in the city. We're the only ones who felt it."

Roxanne rubbed her neck, trying to dispel the uncomfortable feeling that was now slithering down her spine. "Then what was this?"

"A warning," Charles muttered.

She shot him a stunned look. "From the witches of the mark?"

"No, from the ones who want Ilaria dead. And it's my fault they've found us."

~ ~ ~

Charles felt the cold, hard reality of it crash down on him. He'd known that using his own powers to find the witches of the mark would make it easier for the slayers who'd been hunting him and Ilaria for the better part of two decades to find him. The more of their powers—his and Ilaria's—they used too closely together, the more of a risk they ran to send out a strong enough magic signature that could be read by other witches. As long as he'd concealed his and Ilaria's powers and kept moving, the witches who wanted her dead hadn't been able to get a clear reading on him or his niece. But since Ilaria had started coming into her powers, it had been harder to remain concealed. And tonight, his scrying for the witches of the mark and Ilaria's fit had caused the pot to boil over and given their enemies enough to sniff them out. The gig was up.

"I used my powers tonight," he explained to Roxanne, but she wasn't even listening.

She'd already jumped into action, ripping open a hidden panel in the living room that contained an array of weapons. She and Zane were arming themselves, exchanging short instructions.

"Can you shoot?" Zane barked at Charles, ready to toss him a gun and a magazine.

But Charles lifted his hand in refusal. "I won't need a gun. Witches are best fought with witchcraft."

Zane snarled, patting the knife that sat in a holster on his hip. "Even witches die when you stab or shoot 'em." He loaded a semi-automatic. "I'll stick with that."

Next to him Roxanne looked ready for a fight, too. She held a gun in her gloved hand, and grabbed a few throwing stars and tucked them into her pockets.

She looked at him now. "How will they attack?"

Charles approached her. "You'll be outnumbered. Judging by the strength of the shaking I'd say there are at least half a dozen of them out there."

"Backup is already on the way," Roxanne assured him.

"They won't be here in time." By his estimate, the drive from Scanguards' headquarters was at least twenty minutes, if not longer.

"You let us worry about that," Zane cut in.

"All we need to do is hold them off until backup gets here," Roxanne explained and glanced at her colleague. "Grayson can cover the back, you and I will take the front."

"No!" Charles protested. "Grayson has to stay with Ilaria to keep her calm. Once she realizes we're being attacked, the evil will try to rise in her. She'll destroy us all to save herself, and there won't be anything we can do."

He noticed Roxanne's lips trembling, as she looked at him as if he'd lost his mind. "How is it that you're still alive?"

"Because up until now I was still stronger than her. But what will happen shortly will put her over the edge. We can't allow it. If the witches bring the fight inside this house, nobody will be able to stop the evil from rising."

"Fuck!" Zane cursed. "And everybody wonders why I hate witches. Go figure."

Ignoring him, Charles shifted his gaze to Roxanne. "We have to lure them away. It won't be easy, and the ruse will be only temporary. But it might buy us enough time until the cavalry arrives."

Roxanne's eyes widened. "What's your plan?"

"Misdirection."

13

"Ready?" Charles asked ten minutes later, peeking out through the kitchen window that looked out over the backyard and up the steep slope.

"This is never gonna work," Roxanne felt compelled to say, even though Charles had explained his plan in detail. He'd also informed Grayson about what to do once Charles, Roxanne, and Zane were outside.

Though Zane hadn't liked the idea either, he'd voted in favor of it. "Better than being sitting ducks and waiting for them to strike."

More worried about leaving Ilaria alone than about her own safety, Roxanne looked at Charles, hoping to sway him. "What if they immediately see through it? Ilaria will be defenseless."

"They won't." Charles's voice inspired confidence, as did the determined look in his eyes. "Have a little faith in my abilities. Don't you remember what I'm capable of?"

Their gazes locked, and for a few seconds, she remembered the things she'd seen him do before, remembered the power that ran in his veins. "Trust me, love," he murmured so softly that she wondered if he'd actually said it, or if she'd only imagined it.

"It's time," Zane advised. "I can hear them."

Charles put his palm on the top of Roxanne's head and closed his eyes. She felt warmth seeping into her, infusing her, changing her. The feeling ran through her veins, spreading like dye through water, until it had reached all her extremities. All of a sudden, she gasped for air. Took in a breath. Exhaled.

Roxanne opened her eyes and stared at Charles.

"Shit," Zane said in wonder. "You smell like a witch."

"Quickly," Charles ordered. "The illusion won't last long."

Without making a sound, Charles eased the side door open and slid outside into the dark. Roxanne was on his heels, with Zane bringing up the rear. Hidden by high bushes and the trash cans that lined the narrow walkway, they crept along the side of the house toward the steep incline behind it. They reached the end of the yard without incident.

Zane took the lead, running up the hill. Trees and bushes grew on the slope.

"What if they don't see us?" Roxanne whispered to Charles as they started climbing side by side.

"They might not have the sensitive hearing of vampires, but they will sense us: two witches and a vampire trying to get away. They'll take the bait. The question is, how far will we get until they spot us?"

"Not far enough," Zane hissed and whirled around just as flashes of light illuminated the sky above them.

"Shit!" Roxanne cursed and reached for her gun, spinning around as well.

She saw the witches immediately. While their forms were difficult to ascertain in the dark despite her vampire vision, their auras were unmistakable. Roxanne aimed and fired. The bullet should have hit its target, but the witch she'd aimed at had thrown up her arms and sent a blast of energy in its direction, sending it off course.

"Duck!" Charles screamed, just as Roxanne realized that the bullet hadn't just veered off course, but was coming straight back at her.

Roxanne felt an impact, however, it wasn't the bullet that knocked her off her feet but Charles slamming into her side. Together, they rolled down the hill a few yards, until he managed to dig his heels into the ground and stop them from tumbling farther.

Meanwhile shots—subdued by a silencer—fired by Zane from higher up where he was sheltering behind a tree, crackled through the night.

"The entire neighborhood is going to come running," Roxanne ground out. Innocents would get caught in the battle.

Pulling her with him to hide behind an old tree stump leaning against a boulder, Charles said, "They will have thrown up a sound barrier. A spell to hide what's happening here. It's not in their interest to attract attention. All they want is to kill Ilaria."

They dove behind the boulder, narrowly avoiding a spear of fire one of the witches had aimed at them. Roxanne felt the heat singeing the ends of her hair as it passed over her.

"Nice weapons your friends have," she hissed.

"Even you must see they're not my friends," Charles retorted and shoved her behind him. "Stay down."

Before she could stop him, he jumped up with outstretched arms and sent a blast of energy toward the witches. An ear-shattering scream sounded through the night. Roxanne jumped up, her gaze darting past Charles's broad body. The aura of one of the witches lit up like a flame, then extinguished just as quickly. Charles's blast had incinerated her.

But Roxanne could find no satisfaction in the witch's death, because one look down at the bottom of the hill confirmed that they were indeed outnumbered. At least six or seven figures were approaching, starting to climb up the slope. And no matter how many bullets Zane fired from high up, his shots kept missing their intended targets. Roxanne did the same, alternately shooting and tossing throwing stars at them. Without any success. As if they were protected by a shield not even Charles seemed to be able to breach.

Steadily, the witches moved closer. Roxanne glanced around. But there was no place to run or hide. They'd gambled and lost. In a few moments, the witches would have them surrounded and pick them off one by one.

"Promise me something, Roxanne," Charles suddenly murmured next to her.

She whipped her head to look at him, his tone sending a shudder down her spine, when her eyes caught the glare of headlights on the street that wound up to the safe house. She focused her vision. SUVs. Black-out vans.

"They're here." She gripped Charles's shoulder and pointed to the road. He followed her outstretched finger. "Scanguards. They'll be able to attack them from behind."

"Only if I can disrupt the shield the witches have erected around themselves. I'm the only one who can pierce it." All of a sudden, Charles pressed his lips to hers, kissing her fiercely. "Always remember that I love you." Then he jumped out from behind the boulder and charged forward, his arms spread like wings.

"Nooooooo!" Roxanne screamed. This was suicide. But this time she wouldn't allow Charles to leave her. This time she'd go with him wherever he went.

A blast of air tossed her on her ass. She scrambled to get up and searched for Charles. He was already facing the enemy, arrows of electrical charges shooting from his fingertips, raining down on the witches and bouncing off their collective shield. Relentlessly he fired at them in an obvious attempt to weaken them, when he finally sank to his knees.

"Noooo!" Roxanne screamed and jumped up. Hoping her witch aura was still intact and knowing that the witches didn't know what Ilaria looked like, she waved her arms at them. "Come and get me, I'm what you want, you fucking cowards!"

Every eye shot to Roxanne. But she only looked at Charles, who now, even in his weakened state, raised his arms. When tiny sparks appeared on his fingertips, she turned on her heel and ran uphill, knowing it would further distract the witches and lure them in her direction.

"This way," Roxanne heard Zane call out to her, and she changed direction.

Behind her, screams and shouts mingled with gunshots and what sounded like explosions. When she reached the tree where Zane was hidden, she looked over her shoulder.

From high above the property she had the perfect vantage point. Somehow Charles had managed to break the witches' protective shield, allowing Scanguards to attack them from behind. The attack took them by surprise. Six witches against more than a dozen vampires. The odds weren't good for the witches.

"We are the best, aren't we?" Zane chuckled next to her. "Though I must say your man down there isn't too bad either. For a witch, that is."

Her eyes darted to the spot where she'd last seen Charles. He was gone. Panicked, she jumped up, but immediately felt Zane's hand on her arm.

"He's there, to the left. Looking for you."

She spotted him and practically hurtled down the hill, flying into his arms. "Don't ever do that again. That was suicide!"

He caught her and pressed her to him. "I'm still alive." He kissed her hard, then looked over his shoulder to where quiet had suddenly descended. "I have the feeling that Scanguards' final invoice is going to be much higher than anticipated."

She pulled his face back to her. "I might be able to negotiate a discount for you."

"Oh yeah, and what's that gonna cost me?"

"I'm not cheap."

"Never thought you were." He kissed her again. Then he took her hand and they walked down the remainder of the hill to where her colleagues were dealing with the bodies of the witches.

She spotted Samson and walked up to him. "How did you manage to get here so fast?"

"We put a team together the moment Haven got off the phone with you," Samson said. "When he told us the mark on Ilaria was indeed the *Mark of Cain*, we figured you might need backup."

Roxanne looked over her shoulder, explaining to Charles, "This is Samson, my boss."

Charles offered his hand to Samson. "I don't know how to thank you."

Samson shook Charles's hand. "Don't make me regret it." He glanced around, nodding to Zane, who was joining them now. "You alright?"

"Course," Zane replied.

Samson craned his neck, peering past Zane. "And Grayson? I don't see him." Concern crept into his voice.

"He's in the house, protecting Ilaria," Charles said.

"Ilaria? Ahh, shit!" Samson cursed, glaring at Roxanne. "After what Haven told you, you had my son protecting the most dangerous witch in San Francisco? Damn it, Roxanne!"

But Roxanne had no chance to reply, because Samson was already charging into the house. Roxanne ran after him. She caught up with him just as he reached the top of the stairs. Inhaling deeply, he followed his son's scent and ripped the door to Ilaria's bedroom open.

"Samson, please, don't do anything rash!" Roxanne called after him.

Samson froze in the door frame.

Roxanne was there a split second later, peering past his shoulder.

There, in the room lit only by a bedside lamp, Grayson sat in the overstuffed armchair, his gun clutched in one hand, and Ilaria curled up on his lap. Their lips were fused in a passionate kiss, Grayson's free hand caressing her nape, while Ilaria writhed on his lap, her hands exploring his torso. The mark on her back was at peace.

"Ahem," Samson finally said.

Ilaria ripped her lips from Grayson's and shrieked. Grayson instantly raised his gun, but just as quickly, lowered it again.

"It's just my dad, babe," he murmured to Ilaria, calmly stroking her back.

"What the—" Charles barreled into the room. "Didn't I warn you not to—"

Grayson cut him off. "You said to keep her calm." He exchanged a smirk with Ilaria. "And I think I did a pretty good job, didn't I?"

Ilaria's face turned bright red.

Grayson grinned like a Cheshire cat. "I rest my case."

Roxanne couldn't suppress a smile. It appeared that Grayson was just as much of a charmer as his father when he wanted to be.

14

Charles wanted to wipe the self-satisfied grin off the young hybrid's face, but one look at Ilaria's back squashed that notion: Grayson had indeed managed to keep the mark calm by distracting Ilaria throughout the battle that had raged outside. And who was he to deny her that small pleasure? After all, she'd never had the chance to flirt with a young man.

"Why don't we go downstairs, and discuss the situation?" Samson suggested motioning to the hallway. Already halfway out the door, he looked over his shoulder at his son. "And Grayson?"

"Yes, Dad?"

"Behave."

"Don't I always?"

Samson rolled his eyes and marched down the corridor to the stairs.

Charles pointed his index finger at the smug young hybrid. "What your father said." He grunted. "Or you'll learn first-hand what the wrath of a witch feels like."

Grayson took his time to answer. "Yes... sir."

Satisfied, Charles turned and caught Roxanne's unreadable gaze on him. He ushered her out of the room, and side by side they walked downstairs, where several Scanguards staff members were milling about.

"Haven, how long till all the bodies are loaded?" Samson asked a broad-shouldered vampire stomping into the hallway.

"Give us twenty minutes, and the place will look as normal as ever."

Nodding to Haven, Samson lifted his hand to Charles and Roxanne in a gesture to join him. "A word."

"Again, I'm grateful—"

But Charles didn't get any further, because Samson lit into him. "What the fuck were you thinking, keeping from us what we were supposed to protect?" His eyes started to shimmer, indicating the caged vampire beneath the surface. "You could have gotten all of us killed! And to use my son—"

"Your son seems to have no objections," Charles protested.

Samson snarled, flashing his fangs. "Because he's a kid with raging hormones! That doesn't make it right or safe."

"Judging by what I saw, he's no kid."

Samson went toe to toe with him. "The point is: you lied to us. Ilaria is a danger. To all of us." He glanced at Roxanne. "Zane filled in HQ, and Haven and I discussed it on the ride here." He glared back at Charles. "My men will take her into custody until she can safely be transferred to the witches who are capable of handling her. We have underground cells at HQ where she'll be safe."

"Over my dead body," Charles protested. "Nobody puts Ilaria in a cell."

Samson braced his hands on his hips. "We don't have a choice. Grayson may have been able to distract her this once, but nobody knows what will happen next time. I'm not playing fast and loose with my family's and my employees' safety."

Charles was ready to explode with fury. "Then consider yourself fired!" Because he'd never allow Ilaria to be put in what amounted to a dungeon, an underground cell. The skin on his nape began to prickle uncomfortably. The thought alone gave him the creeps.

"Too late! You don't get to fire us. This is a matter of protecting our own now."

The prickling grew stronger, and something else did, too, the awareness that he and Ilaria weren't the only witches in the house anymore. Had one of the enemy witches managed to hide? Were they about to be ambushed?

"Witch!" Charles screamed and whirled around.

Several weapons were instantly leveled at the figure standing in the open front door.

"Don't shoot!" Charles screamed, throwing himself between the pointed guns and the witch. "I know her."

But he shouldn't have bothered, because the witch who he'd spoken to at Golden Gate Park only hours earlier threw her hand up and shielded herself with her own power, the force field protecting her so strong that the air between her and the vampires shimmered with a silvery glow.

The Scanguards men didn't stand down.

"It's touching that you want to protect me," the witch drawled in much the same tone she had employed earlier in the woods. "But I need no protection from vampires." She stepped past him, motioning to Samson. "You look like you're their leader."

Samson nodded.

"I mean you no harm. I'm here for the girl." She cast a glance toward the back side of the house. "Given what happened here tonight, my coven has voted to take her in immediately. Better for all of us. Don't you agree?"

"If she agrees to go with you, my men won't stop you," Samson said.

On the stairs, Charles heard footsteps. He looked over his shoulder. Ilaria had put on a sweater and jeans and was walking toward them. She, too, had sensed the arrival of the witch of the mark. When Ilaria reached the bottom of the stairs, Charles took her hand.

"Are you ready for this?"

She smiled and glanced at the stranger. "I've always been ready." Then she looked back to the top of the stairs, where Grayson stood, his hands in his pockets, a solemn expression on his face.

"Thank you," Ilaria whispered, her voice thick with tears.

Charles squeezed her hand and she met his eyes. "I will miss you, sweetheart."

Ilaria threw her arms around him. "I'll miss you, too, Uncle Charles."

In that moment he felt like more than just an uncle, he felt like a father who was losing his daughter. As if Ilaria felt it, she looked up and locked eyes with him. "One day, we'll meet again. Promise me you won't worry about me. It's time you lived your own life now. You've sacrificed so much of it already."

Involuntarily, his gaze drifted away from Ilaria to Roxanne, who stood between her colleagues. She'd lowered her weapon, though her colleagues were still pointing theirs at the witch.

"Come, my child." The witch of the mark stretched out her hand, and without hesitation or fear Ilaria took it and allowed the stranger to lead her away.

Relieved breaths filled the room, mixing with the muffled clicks of guns being put back on safety and holstered. The threat was finally over.

Charles felt the tension roll off Samson.

"Let's get the hell out of here, guys," Samson said to his men. He glanced at Roxanne. "You leaving with us?"

Charles caught the look that Roxanne slanted him, before she answered her boss's question. "There's something I need to do first. I'll see you all at headquarters tomorrow night."

Samson nodded in agreement.

A few minutes later, all of Roxanne's colleagues had left and taken all the evidence that a fight had taken place here with them.

He and Roxanne were finally alone.

15

Roxanne watched Charles close the door behind her colleagues and turn the deadbolt. When he turned around, she met his gaze.

She didn't really know how to start, what to say, what to do, but she knew it was her turn. She felt it.

"When I saw Ilaria's mark, when I saw it pulse, I finally understood why you did what you did. Why you left me."

He reached out his hand. "I never wanted to."

"You had no choice. Without you, Ilaria would have never survived to adulthood. And you did it knowing that any moment she could turn on you and allow the evil inside her to destroy you."

She saw his eyes grow moist, and he said, "Because I knew that if I could deliver Ilaria to safety, then I would be allowed to return to you. If you could forgive me for what I did."

Slowly, she shook her head. "Forgive you?"

He dropped his head.

"Oh Charles, there's nothing to forgive." Roxanne crossed the distance between them and wrapped her arms around him, feeling him shudder with relief. "I only wish you would have allowed me to be by your side. We would have been even stronger together."

His hands were on her face then, tilting it up to him. "I know that now. Having seen how you showed no fear toward her, I realize that I was wrong. But I couldn't take the risk, not knowing what raising a witch of the mark would entail. I couldn't risk your life. I loved you too much. I still do."

"I tried to stop loving you," Roxanne murmured, tears brimming at her eyes. "But I failed."

"Nobody's perfect. Not even you." Charles chuckled, and the sound pierced her heart, tearing down the wall that she'd built around it. "And that's exactly the way I love you."

She laughed through the tears that now rolled down her cheeks. She didn't have to hide them any longer. "I love you, Charles."

In the next instant he'd lifted her up and was carrying her toward the stairs.

"What are you doing?"

"Taking you to bed, my love."

"But I'm not tired," she teased him, feeling warmth bubble up in her.

"Neither am I."

Upstairs, Charles pushed the door to the bedroom open and flipped the light switch. He froze, and Roxanne took her eyes off him and let her gaze roam.

The room looked as if it had been cut out from a honeymoon magazine. A large bed with a white muslin canopy dominated the room. Soft sheets covered the mattress. The harsh ceiling light had been replaced by two bedside lamps that gave off an orange glow.

And though she knew it was only an illusion, she murmured, "It's beautiful. Thank you."

Charles met her eyes. "Don't thank me. I have a feeling this is a goodbye present from Ilaria."

"Then how about we play with our present? I'm sure she would want that."

Charles winked at her. "I agree."

He lowered her onto the bed and began to undress. She watched him, growing hungry at the sight of him. First, he revealed a nearly hairless chest with toned muscles. His biceps were pronounced. They flexed as he pulled his Polo-shirt over his head. He tossed it on the floor, then popped the button of his pants open, and lifted his gaze.

He chuckled. "This game is only gonna work if we're both naked."

"I was only admiring what'll become mine soon." And soon couldn't come quickly enough. "I'm playing for keeps this time."

~ ~ ~

Charles's heart flipped. He'd dreamed of this moment for so many years: to hear Roxanne tell him that she wanted to spend eternity with him.

He wasted no time and undressed until he stood before her naked, his cock already hard, heavy, and impatient. He stood there at the foot of the bed for a moment, looking down at Roxanne and how she licked her lips while feasting her eyes on him.

"The sooner you get undressed, the quicker you'll get what you crave," he said, running his eyes over her.

"I didn't want to miss anything," she said, then started to undress.

First her top fell to the floor, then her shoes and pants. His mouth was watering when she unhooked her bra and slid it off, but when her thumbs hooked into her G-string, pushing it down over her legs, he felt his cock jerk in anticipation.

They were both bare tonight, not only physically, but emotionally.

Charles slid one knee onto the mattress, bracing himself above her. She reached for him, her hands pulling his head down to hers, her eyes shimmering golden now. He'd always thought her beautiful, but whenever he saw her irises light up with the fire of her vampire side, he felt a primal hunger awaken in him. One only Roxanne could still.

He took her lips, kissing her for the first time without any lies or secrets between them. Roxanne eagerly lapped against him, the forceful pressing of her tongue against his reminding him how strong she was. How powerful. And how different from him. He—a witch loving the light. She—a vampire living in darkness.

Yet as he kissed her passionately and explored her with his hands, reacquainting himself with her luscious curves and her silken skin, he knew they were meant for each other. Meant to bridge the differences between their species by allowing the love and trust between them to flourish.

With every second, the kiss turned more urgent. He felt Roxanne pull him into her center, making his cock slide to the juncture at her thighs, where warmth and moisture had gathered. He rubbed his cockhead along her slit and groaned at the smooth contact. Underneath him, Roxanne twisted, shifting to angle her pelvis.

The tip of his cock pushed between the swollen lips of her sex.

"Fuck!" he cursed, ripping his mouth from hers and throwing his head back. "Too good!"

He had no self-control, no patience. As much as he wanted to slow this down, he couldn't stop himself and plunged into her hot, wet pussy. Roxanne welcomed him, her legs already wrapping around him so he couldn't escape, her fingernails digging into his flesh. He'd always loved that, always loved how she let go of all restraints when he was inside her. How she gave herself to him as if he were the stronger of them, when he knew she could kill him with her sharp claws and fangs. Yet, he'd never felt any fear, because love made them equals. Love gave him power over her, just as she had power over him.

But tonight they would even surpass all that, because tonight, they would truly become one.

He rode her hard, thrusting deep and fast, moving in ways he knew drove her wild. She hadn't changed at all, still released the same sighs she always had, when he rubbed her clit just right. It was thrilling to watch her body erupt in pleasure, but to take part in it, to feel her interior muscles clamp around him, contracting and releasing, was more than any man could ever dream of. He was one lucky son-of-a-bitch to have earned the love of a woman like Roxanne.

"Make me yours," he demanded, not being able to wait any longer. Patience was overrated. They had all eternity together. Maybe he'd learn patience then, but he'd waited twenty-three years for this, and he didn't want to wait a moment longer.

Roxanne's eyes flashed and their golden shimmer turned orange and then red. The tips of her fangs pushed past her lips, descending to their full length. She brought her hand to her shoulder, and he watched in fascination how she sliced into her skin. Blood dripped from the incision.

He met her eyes then and saw the hunger in them. And the love. The trust. Because once they completed the bond, Roxanne would only drink from him. He would become her only source of nourishment. And he wanted this responsibility. Craved it in fact.

"Be mine," he murmured and pressed his lips to the tiny wound on Roxanne's shoulder, lapping up the blood that seeped from it, and sucking from it to demand more.

He felt her shudder beneath him, her muscles spasming as her climax rocked her. Then he felt it. She drove her sharp fangs into his neck, piercing his vein. He trembled with pleasure and let go of the last threads of his control. His orgasm slammed into him like a wave crashing against a cliff.

Oh God, how he'd missed her bite. How had he survived without it, without her, for so long? He'd been more dead than alive and he hadn't even realized it.

I know. It was Roxanne's voice in his head.

He was prepared for it, had known that this would happen, that he and Roxanne would have a telepathic connection forged by the bond. But he could have never imagined how intense it was, how close he would feel to her, how much of her heart and soul he would feel seeping into him.

I'll never leave you, my love, he responded in the same way she'd sent her thoughts to him.

I'll chase you to the end of the earth if you do. And I'm faster than you.

He wanted to chuckle at that and, were he not so busy drinking Roxanne's blood, while she drank his, he would have. Instead, he gave her the only response he could think of.

He made love to her until neither of them could move another limb.

When they finally stopped moving, he pulled her into the curve of his body, her back to his chest, and used what was left of his energy to cast one spell.

Invisible tendrils like silk ties grew around them, binding them together.

"Oh Charles," Roxanne murmured sleepily and sighed.

He nuzzled his face in the crook of her neck. "I've got you now. And I'll never let go."

~ ~ ~

Mortal Wish is a work of fiction. Names, characters, places, and incidents are the products of the author's imagination and are used fictitiously. Any resemblance to actual events, locales, or persons, living or dead, is entirely coincidental.

2013 – 2016 Tina Folsom

Published in the United States

Cover design: Leah Kaye Suttle
Cover photo: 123RF.com

Printed in the United States of America

MORTAL WISH

SCANGUARDS VAMPIRES
(A PREQUEL NOVELLA)

TINA FOLSOM

1

On an island in the Gulf of Mexico, December 1991

Jake watched the man as he tied the ferry to the boat dock, then proceeded to move the gangplank over the gap between dock and ferry and secure it tightly, before he hollered to the captain, "Boat's tied up."

The captain waved back, then shifted his gaze to Jake. "Have a pleasant stay."

Jake walked over the gangplank and onto the dock. He'd been the only passenger on the evening ferry. He assumed that most visitors descending upon this tiny island of barely one thousand inhabitants had done so with an earlier ferry, but he hadn't had a choice. Traveling during daylight hours was impossible for him.

"Mr. Stone?"

At a voice calling his name, he turned his head and noticed a gangly kid who couldn't be more than twenty years old waving at him from next to the harbor master's hut. The boy's red hair was like a beacon in the night, as was the scent that came from him: fresh, young blood.

Luckily, Jake had fed plenty before his departure from the mainland, not wanting to be caught hunting on the small island. He'd also packed blood he'd stolen from a blood bank in New York where he'd lived during the last year. There, anonymity had been his friend, whereas in small towns people looked out for each other and would interfere when they saw something odd happening—like him sucking on the neck of a juicy human.

"I'm Jake Stone," he called out as he approached the kid, whose blood smelled pure and rich, and just a tad too inviting.

When he stopped before the youngster, holding his overnight bag in one hand, the kid gave him a wide smile. "I'm Carl. Welcome to Seeker's Island. Mrs. Adams sent me. I'll take you to the Sunseekers Inn."

Carl made a motion for the bag, but Jake didn't relinquish it. "Lead the way."

The kid gestured to the street that ran alongside the small harbor. "I'm parked right here."

Jake arched an eyebrow. He hadn't expected this island to allow cars. "Where?"

Carl pointed toward a white object that stood at the curb.

"A golf cart," Jake murmured. *With a sprig of mistletoe dangling from its rearview mirror?*

The kid nodded enthusiastically. "We don't have cars on the island. But I get to use one of the golf carts to drive tourists around. I mean, it's practically mine."

Jake forced a smile and followed him. Great: Carl was a chatterbox. That was just what he needed. If he'd had a choice, he wouldn't have come to a small island like this where everybody knew everybody else's business, but he hadn't had a choice. This was his last resort.

As Jake slunk into the passenger seat and set his bag between his feet, Carl started the electric engine and pulled into the street that ran alongside the coast. Houses and shops lined the quaint road and made him feel like he'd entered Disneyland. Well, Disneyland decked out for Christmas—because practically every store and restaurant was decorated with colorful lights, red and green being the dominant ones. And maybe this island was just like Disneyland, full of make believes and wishes for things he couldn't have.

"Are you here for the... you know?" Carl continued.

Knowing that the kid was referring to the hot spring that was said to have magical qualities, Jake gave no direct answer and instead let his eyes wander toward the ocean and the impenetrable darkness beyond the shore. "The... you know what... doesn't really work, does it?"

Carl sat up taller as if wanting to display more authority. "Of course it does!" Then he lowered his voice and leaned closer, whispering now. "I grew up here. Everything you've heard is true. If you drink from it, you'll get your heart's desire."

Jake suppressed the urge to scoff. If the spring really worked, why was a young man like Carl still living here, performing the thankless job of chauffeuring tourists around the island? "Sure, whatever you say."

Maybe he was just cynical—what one-hundred-forty-seven year old vampire wouldn't be? Or maybe he was simply bracing himself for the moment when he found out that the magical spring didn't actually have the power to grant any wishes.

"You'll see!" Carl prophesied and brought the cart to a stop. He pointed to the large Victorian house that stood behind a white picket fence. "We're here."

Jake pulled a five dollar bill from his pocket and handed it to the kid. "Thanks, Carl."

The youngster grinned as he pocketed the money. "And if you need any transportation on the island, I'm happy to drive you around."

Jake had no doubt about that. He was sure that opportunities for making money on the island were few and far between. "I'll let you know." He got out of the cart and walked up the entrance way to the house, bag in hand.

The electric engine made barely any sound when Carl left.

Jake opened the entrance door and entered. The foyer was cozy and well lit. A large Christmas tree adorned with antique ornaments took up half the entry hall. He had to admit—despite his aversion to Christmas—that the fresh blue spruce looked rather pretty, and the scent brought back memories of his childhood. Memories of happier times.

A large wooden staircase led to the upper floors. To its left was a reception area, which looked like a booth with a high counter in front and shelves at the back. He approached it and set his bag on the floor. Seeing nobody, but sensing he wasn't alone, he hit the little bell on the counter.

As the soft ping chimed through the foyer, he suddenly heard a sound and an instant later, a woman rose from behind the counter, righting the sleeve of her colorful dress, while giving him an apologetic smile. He hadn't seen her earlier, nor had his senses picked up on her smell. The scent of the fresh tree, the potpourri, and the scented candles that seemed to be wherever there was a ledge or an available surface, was too overwhelming.

"Oh, dear, you've caught me now!" She chuckled and blushed furiously. "Those darn straps, they never stay in place." She pulled her hand out from under her sleeve and adjusted her scoop neck.

Jake could only imagine that she was talking about her bra straps and tried not to focus on her ample chest. Instead, he looked at her face. She was still attractive even though she seemed to be in her early sixties. Had he met her twenty or thirty years ago, he would have seduced her.

"Mrs. Adams?"

"Yes, and you must be Mr. Stone." She let her eyes roam over his face and body, not hiding the fact that she found him attractive.

He was used to those looks. He got them from women of all ages. But all they saw was his perfect shell: the dark hair, the chiseled chin, the classical nose, the piercing blue eyes, and the sculpted body. What they didn't see was the man inside, the man who yearned for a real life, for a mortal life. For a purpose.

"I have a wonderful room for you. On the top floor. It's got a gorgeous view of the bay on the other side of the island." She reached for the board of keys behind her and took one of them down, placing it on the counter.

"Perfect." He smiled and grabbed the key.

"Breakfast is included." She pointed toward a door next to the stairs. "The breakfast room is through here. We serve breakfast from seven till nine thirty."

"That won't be necessary. I'm not much of a morning person. In fact, would you mind if I declined housekeeping? I'm quite a night owl actually and sleep really late." Late as in *until sunset*. After all, daylight didn't agree with him. The charred look had never appealed to him.

"Oh?" She cast him a surprised glance. "I hope you won't be too disappointed about the nightlife here, but there's practically none. A lot of our visitors are here for the hot spring." She leaned forward, her boobs resting on the counter as she did so. "I assume you came for the same thing?"

Jake sighed. He'd been here for less than half an hour and already two people had managed to ask him the same question. But being the intensely private man he was, he had no intention of getting dragged into a conversation about his very personal desires. Desires he could share with nobody.

"I hear fishing is good out here."

A disappointed frown spread over Mrs. Adams' face as she straightened. "Yes, yes, it is."

"Top floor, you said?" He pointed toward the stairs and picked up his bag, not waiting for her answer.

"Number twenty-one. Turn left at the top of the stairs."

The stairs creaked as he walked up the first flight. Runners covered the worn floors on the landing. Jake let his eyes wander over the old paintings on the walls and the antique sideboard that adorned the second floor hallway. His eyes lingered on the fine workmanship for a moment longer, then he already continued around the banister.

He ran into something soft. His head jerked around, and his hand released the grip on his bag in the same moment that he instinctively reached for the person he'd run into. His eyes perceived a woman, her arms flailing, releasing the handbag she carried. As its contents spilled onto the floor, Jake caught the woman, preventing her from falling.

"Ooops!" he called out. "Gotcha!"

"Uhh!"

She breathed heavily, and his superior senses picked up her elevated heartbeat.

"I'm so sorry, I didn't look," he apologized.

"That's quite all right," she answered breathlessly. "It's my own fault. I was running around the corner without looking." She eased from his grip and stepped back.

Jake's eyes fell on her face. Her eyes were just as blue as his, and her long hair was of a rich auburn shade. Her skin was flawless, but pale, almost like porcelain, and it made her lips look as red as fresh blood. Hunger surged within him instantly, despite the fact that he was sated. He pushed it back. Instead he looked to the items that had fallen to the floor and bent down.

"Let me help you with this," he offered and handed her the handbag.

She took it and crouched down opposite him, quickly picking up some of the fallen items: a lipstick, keys, a small notepad.

Jake handed her a handkerchief and a pen, then searched the rug for anything else that might have fallen out, but found nothing.

"I think I've got everything," she said and rose.

He got up from his hunched position and offered his hand in greeting. "I'm Jake, by the way."

She hesitated, before she shook his hand very briefly. "Claire." Then she motioned to the stairs. "I've gotta go."

He watched as she hurried down the stairs. Her footsteps echoed in the foyer as she rushed out the entrance door. Only when it fell shut with a loud thud did he pick up his own bag and proceed to his room.

2

After a refreshing shower, Jake left his room. It was time to do what he'd come here for. No need to drag out the inevitable. He walked down the first flight of stairs, reaching the spot where he'd run into the very enticing Claire. For a moment, he stopped there. She'd stirred something in him, awakening a sense of wanting to protect her, even though he'd never felt that way toward a human. He'd always been the predator, taking what he wanted, not caring whom he hurt. But it was all different now.

He was done being the monster they feared. He was done with this life. Too many kills lay in his past, too many bad deeds lined his path. The senselessness of it all had come full circle. His life had no meaning; he understood that now after having lived as a vampire for one-hundred-twelve years, after having been turned at the age of thirty-five.

He couldn't do it any longer: he couldn't hurt people any longer. Because he'd developed a conscience. A fucking conscience!

He stared at his shoes and cursed silently. Who'd ever heard of a vampire with scruples? But no, he had to suddenly want a meaningful life, a purpose. And he knew there was only one way to have a meaningful life: he had to become human again.

His discontent with his life as a vampire had come gradually. Every time he'd watched humans celebrate another milestone in their lives, a new love, a wedding, or a birth, he'd felt himself grow more envious. And he'd started comparing his miserable life to theirs and found it lacking. There were no joyful events in his life: he slept, he hunted, he fed. And he was always hiding. But most of all, he had nobody who cared for him or whom he cared about. Tender emotions were foreign to him. Yet he recognized them in others, in humans, and he wanted to feel the same. And if he couldn't achieve that, then he'd rather not feel anything at all.

That's why he'd come to the island: to drink the water of the hot spring and wish for his heart's desire. And if the legendary spring failed him, then there was only one other thing to do. If he had the courage to do it.

He let out a bitter laugh when he noticed an object beneath the sideboard he'd admired earlier. Out of curiosity, he bent down and reached for it. His fingers closed around a transparent orange colored prescription bottle. He read the label on it and froze.

It belonged to a Claire Culver—the woman he'd bumped into. The pill bottle must have fallen out of her bag and rolled under the sideboard, and they had both overlooked it. He read the name of the medication. Since as a vampire he wasn't susceptible to any diseases, he wasn't familiar with the name, even though he remembered having heard it on a TV program. What had it been for? He searched his brain, but couldn't recall it.

Chastising himself for his inappropriate curiosity, he continued down the stairs. It was none of his business what medication Claire took and what it was for. She was a stranger to him and would remain a stranger.

When he reached the foyer, Mrs. Adams was pulling the curtains shut in the hallway. She turned to him.

"Out for a nightcap?" she asked.

"Yeah, I figured I'd explore that nightlife you were talking about earlier." He winked at her and enjoyed the fact that she blushed once more.

"Luke runs a Tiki bar not far from here. You might want to try that," she suggested.

"Sounds right up my alley." He rolled the pill bottle between his fingers. "Oh, and Mrs. Adams, I found this on the floor upstairs. It belongs to Miss Culver. She must have dropped it." He handed it to her and decided not to tell her that he was the reason it had fallen out of Claire's handbag. "Would you please give it to her when you see her?"

"Oh, dear." Mrs. Adams sighed heavily, making him pause for a moment.

"Something wrong?"

"Well," she started, "such a shame. And she's so young and pretty, too. Has her whole life ahead of her, except she doesn't."

A cold shiver crept up his spine. "Excuse me?"

She motioned to the medication. "Miss Culver." She took a step closer and lowered her voice. "I shouldn't tell you this, but since you found her medication, you'd probably be able to figure it out yourself anyway. I only know because she had a seizure the other day, and I had to call the doctor, and he's my cousin's husband. And you know, she told me. My cousin, that is. Because her husband told her."

Jake took a deep breath, hesitating for a second. Should he stay and allow her to divulge private medical information about Claire? Wouldn't it be better, if he simply walked away and didn't get involved? But Mrs. Adams had mentioned seizures, and that word had piqued his interest.

"Yes?"

She leaned in. "Brain cancer. Apparently she got diagnosed six months ago. It's inoperable. The doctors have given her another few weeks or months." She pointed to the pills. "She takes those to keep the pain at bay. But the seizures continue. The doctors have given up. That's why she's here. You know, for the hot spring."

He nodded, shocked at the revelation. No wonder Claire had looked so pale. Had he sensed her illness? Was that why he'd had the feeling that she needed protection? "She's come to wish for a cure."

A sad smile played around Mrs. Adams' lips. "Several times a day, she goes there. She's there now. And on the way back she stops at the bar and drowns her sorrows. And tomorrow she'll do the same thing again. It's so sad to watch."

"So the hot spring doesn't have any real power, does it?"

"Oh, it does, but sometimes we're not wishing for the right thing. Sometimes we don't know what our heart's true desire is. And the spring only grants those desires that are pure and true."

"What could be purer than wanting a cure for her cancer?" he wondered.

"I'm not saying that her desires are not pure. But sometimes the spring just needs a sacrifice to work," she answered cryptically.

Visions of slaughtered animals popped into his head. But he was sure that Mrs. Adams was talking about other kinds of sacrifices.

"Maybe you just want to tell Miss Culver that you found the pill bottle yourself. There's no need for her to think that I know what's going on. I'm sure she values her privacy."

Without waiting for her response, he left the house and turned toward the main road on his search for the Tiki bar. After the information Mrs. Adams had shared with him, he wasn't in the right frame of mind to visit the spring right now.

3

Claire cast one last look back at the hot spring. When she'd arrived over an hour earlier, she'd captured some fresh water from where it poured out of the rocks with her cupped palms and swallowed it. At the same time she'd prayed for a miracle. Just like she'd done in the past five days since she'd come to the island. So far, nothing had changed. Her headaches were as painful as ever and were only subdued by the strong painkillers her oncologist had prescribed. But even those didn't dull the pain for long. So she'd started drinking in the evenings to drown out the pounding in her head.

With each day that passed, hope faded further into the background as reality pushed to the forefront. Science had given up on her long ago, and the miracle she was hoping for by making the same wish at the spring over and over again wasn't happening. In a few days the pain would be so excruciating and the seizures so severe that she would most likely fall into a coma from which she would never wake. Her time was up.

As she walked back on the dirt path that led into the village, she reflected on her life. But looking back on it made what lay ahead of her even harder to bear. She wasn't ready to die. There was so much she hadn't done, hadn't seen, hadn't experienced. It just wasn't fair. She'd been a good person, honest, reliable, decent through and through. She'd never hurt anybody.

Like the other nights before, she headed for the Tiki bar. Some alcohol would numb her mind and stop her from speculating whether things would have turned out differently if only she'd gone to the doctor earlier when her headaches had started. She didn't want to think about things she couldn't change.

When she approached the bar, she already saw that it was half full like the night before: there were no walls. A bar stood in the middle of a hut without walls, its shutters, which protected the liquor from theft during the day, lifted and secured to the ceiling during opening hours. Soft music came from the speakers. One couple, embracing, danced slowly on the tiny makeshift dance floor. Others sat at the tables or at the bar, drinking and talking. Laughing. She steered for the bar and took the only vacant bar stool next to a tall dark haired man whose back was turned to her as he watched a football game on the muted TV that hung from the ceiling.

Claire motioned to the owner. He'd introduced himself the first night. "Evening, Luke."

"Hi Claire. The usual?"

She nodded and watched how he prepared her Whiskey Sour the way she liked it. Might as well go out in style, she figured. When he put it in front of her, she lifted her glass to her lips and took the first sip.

The man next to her turned. "Cheers."

She almost choked and quickly set the glass back on the counter. The man next to her was Jake, who she'd crashed into as she was running down the stairs at the Bed and Breakfast.

"Oh!" Just like earlier, she was unable to form a coherent sentence.

This time she couldn't blame her monosyllabic response on the fact that they'd bumped into each other. No, she had to admit that she was tongue-tied because Jake exuded such pure maleness that her entire body was bursting into flames. She'd had her share of boyfriends, of course, good looking ones, too, but she'd never been with a man like the one who now gazed at her with such intensity that she wanted to rip her clothes from her body and offer herself to him.

Good God! What was she thinking? She was clearly going mad. Yes, she was finally slipping into insanity, unable to control her mind.

"Hi," she said quickly before the silence between them stretched any longer. "Guess this is the only bar in town." She sounded silly in her own ears, but Jake smiled at her nevertheless.

"Not much of a nightlife here on the island, I gather. Besides, it's off season. But I suppose that's not why people come here." He gave her an expectant look.

"Have you been to the hot spring?" she asked him and took another sip from her drink so that her hands had something to do and he wouldn't notice that they trembled.

"Not yet. I'm not in a rush. It'll be there when I'm ready."

She stared at the bottles that were lined up on the shelves suspended over the bar, nodding in agreement. "Still figuring out what you want?"

He shook his head. "I know what I want."

Claire was surprised at herself. She wasn't one to start a candid conversation with a stranger, but oddly enough, his openness was inviting her to talk as if they'd known each other for a while. Maybe it was because they were two lonely strangers in a bar, both with a wish they wanted fulfilled. Even though she couldn't imagine what Jake could possibly wish for: didn't a man like him have everything? Looks, strength, power? Women throwing themselves at his feet?

"Do you believe in it?" she heard herself ask.

"The hot spring?"

She nodded.

"I don't know what to believe."

"Is that why you're waiting?" She turned her head to look at him.

His blue eyes locked with hers. "Is that why you're going every day? Because you don't know whether to believe in it?"

Her breath hitched. "You seem to know an awful lot." If she were in a large city, she would be worried about him being a stalker. However, she knew how things on this island worked: nothing stayed a secret for longer than five minutes.

Jake shrugged, then took a sip from his red wine. "The islanders seem to keep a close eye on who's visiting the hot spring."

"They're very protective of it," she agreed and downed the rest of her drink in one big gulp. She made a gesture to get down from her barstool, when she suddenly felt his hand on her forearm.

"Don't leave," he said quietly. "I didn't mean to scare you off."

She hesitated, staring at his hand, then lifted her gaze to his face. His eyes were warm. She allowed herself to get drawn into their blue depths.

"Dance with me," Jake whispered.

"I... uh," she started.

"What have you got to lose? It's just a dance between two strangers. I'll be gone in a couple of days, and you'll never have to see me again."

He was right. She had nothing to lose. And why shouldn't she allow herself to sway with the rhythm of the music, a stranger's arms holding her for a few minutes, making her forget her sorrows?

"One dance," Claire agreed.

"One dance," he repeated and with ease lifted her from her barstool.

A moment later, she found herself on the dance floor, his arms holding her close to him, his thighs brushing hers, his hand on the small of her back pressing her closer to his torso, so she could feel his body heat engulf her. She closed her eyes and let herself fall into the dream that her life was only just beginning. That it wouldn't end.

4

Jake pulled her closer and moved to the rhythm of the music. He hadn't danced in a long time, but the steps were ingrained in him nevertheless. He'd always loved dancing, always loved the feeling of holding a woman in his arms.

Pressing his cheek to hers, he spoke softly. "I heard that sometimes the hot spring needs a sacrifice to grant a wish."

Claire pulled her face back to look at him. "Who told you that?"

"Mrs. Adams."

She leaned back into him. "She never mentioned anything to me about that."

"Maybe you're not the one to offer a sacrifice." Maybe Mrs. Adams had meant this only for him—without knowing what his wish was—because he was the one asking for the impossible, and his wish demanded a sacrifice.

"What if it's all a lie?" she mused. "What if the spring does nothing? What will you do then?"

"What will *I* do?"

"Yes, you. If you found out tonight that the spring doesn't work, what would you do tomorrow?"

He'd thought about it ever since he'd decided to come to the island. "I would go to the beach and wait there until the sun rose." He wouldn't seek shelter from it, but allow the sun to turn him into dust and the ocean surf to sweep his remains away as if he'd never existed.

"Yes, your life would just go on. I wish it were the same for me."

Jake didn't correct her assumption. He heard the rising tears in Claire's voice, but he wouldn't allow her to cry. Not as long as she was with him. At least for tonight he wanted her to feel joy and pleasure.

"Come to the beach with me, now. And I'll make you forget the things you want to forget. Just for tonight. Just you and me. The world around us doesn't exist. The spring doesn't exist."

She didn't pull away from him despite his outrageous offer. Instead he felt her nod. "Yes, make me forget, just for a little while." Then she lifted her head and looked at him. "You must think me easy."

He moved his head from side to side. "Do you think *me* easy?"

Clearly surprised at his question, she shook her head. "No."

"Then why would I find *you* easy? Just because you allow yourself to say yes to something you want? I don't judge people who follow their desires." Jake lowered his head until his lips hovered over hers. "You still have a chance to change your mind, but once I kiss you—"

He didn't get an opportunity to finish his sentence, because Claire leaned in and kissed him. Stunned and elated at the same time he savored her soft lips for an altogether too-brief moment, before she pulled back again.

"I won't change my mind." Her whispered words blew against his face.

Without waiting for the song to end, he led her toward the bar, tossed a twenty on it and left without another word. It didn't matter what the bartender thought of them. Finding his bearings, he turned into the next side street and headed northwest.

The beach was deserted. And just like he'd thought he'd seen from his bedroom window, there was a small shed. He approached it and read the sign on it: *Beach Rentals*. A small padlock denied access to the contents of the shed. He reached for the lock.

"What are you doing? You're not going to break in, are you?"

He winked at her. "Let's live on the wild side for tonight." Then he moved so she couldn't see how he was opening the lock: with pure vampire strength.

The shed contained what he was looking for: cushions for the lounge chairs that were neatly stacked up next to the shed. He pulled two of them out and spread them in the sand, creating a makeshift bed.

When he caught her still stunned look, he put his arm around her waist and drew her against his body. "Trust me; we'll both be more comfortable that way."

"I'm not looking for comfortable." Her lids swung open, her lashes almost crashing into her eyebrows.

God, she was beautiful. It hit him right there—that this beauty would be gone from this world very soon. That knowledge squeezed his heart like an iron fist clamping around it. The pain was palpable even though he shouldn't feel any physical pain.

Jake brought his lips to hers, almost touching them, but not quite. "What are you looking for?"

"To feel alive."

"Just alive? I can do better than that, darling."

Her lips were soft and yielding when he slid his mouth over them and captured them gently. There was no hurry. The sun wouldn't rise for another seven hours. He had time to make leisurely love to her. To give her everything she needed, just so she would feel cherished once more.

Claire wore a light dress, and pressed against his short-sleeved cotton shirt and his linen pants, he could feel every curve of her body. She wasn't voluptuous by any stretch of the imagination, but she was well proportioned. Pulling her closer, he slipped his hand onto her backside, palming the alluring swell.

A soft moan issued from her throat. He swallowed it just as her lips opened, allowing him to sweep her tongue inside to explore her. Tasting her sweet essence, his body hardened, one appendage more so than the rest of his body: his cock, while already semi-erect when he'd danced with her, now surged to its fully erect state.

He couldn't resist and pressed his hips more firmly into her soft center, letting her feel what she'd done to him. In response, she lowered her hands down to his backside. He could feel her fingernails digging themselves hard into his flesh, a feeling he welcomed more than she could know.

He'd always loved it when his vampire lovers had dug their claws into him, drawing blood while he drove his cock into them. He wished for the same thing now, for some fierce lovemaking, a no-holds-barred experience.

His fangs began to itch at the very thought of it, and he could feel them lengthen. Desperate to keep his vampire side from emerging, he ripped his mouth from hers and lifted her off her feet. Then he lowered her to lie on the lounge cushions he'd spread out.

He searched for the zipper of her dress and lowered it. Like a shy virgin, she looked away, but he wouldn't have any of it.

"Claire," he prompted her, drawing her gaze back onto him. "I want you to watch me undress."

He noticed her swallow hard. But she said nothing. Slowly, he opened the buttons of his shirt, then shed the garment. Her eyes danced to his chest. She pulled her lower lip between her teeth, showing him her appreciation. When her gaze dropped to his pants, his heart suddenly beat faster. Claire was looking at the bulge that had formed behind the zipper, all shyness gone now.

When she licked her lips, he groaned involuntarily.

Jake opened his pants and stepped out of them, leaving him only with his boxer briefs. They stretched tightly over his ever-growing erection. When he looked down at himself, he noticed that a drop of moisture had oozed from it and was showing through the fabric.

He was sure she saw it, too, the moonlight providing sufficient light even for a human's eyes to see. Standing above her, he hooked his thumbs into the waistband of his boxer briefs then shoved them lower until he'd freed his cock. Cool night air blew against his hard-on, but it did nothing to quell the raging organ.

Claire was still staring at him, her eyes wide, her lips parted, when he rid himself of the garment. Her chest heaved, and he could see her hard nipples press through the fabric of her dress.

"Now you. Undress for me."

He lowered himself onto his knees, close enough so nothing would escape his watchful eye.

With hesitant movements she pushed one strap off her shoulders, revealing creamy skin, then she dropped the second one and pulled on the fabric, exposing more of her skin. The top of her breasts came into view, then a second later, the perfectly round mounds topped with hard rosy nipples lay bare.

Jake sucked in a gulp of air. "You're beautiful. So perfect."

Encouraged by his words, she pushed the fabric lower. When she reached her hips, she paused.

"Show me more," he demanded.

Claire pushed the dress below her hips and freed herself from it. She wore the tiniest panties he'd seen in a long time, the triangle of fabric barely covering her dark nest of hair, the strings holding it up so thin, he knew if he touched them, he would rip the garment to shreds. And that was exactly what he wanted to do.

When her hand went to her panties, he stopped her. "Wait."

She gave him a startled look. "I thought you wanted me to undress."

"I've changed my mind." He went onto his hands and knees and crawled closer. "I want to do the rest myself, unless you object."

She leaned back with a smile. "I don't object."

For a long moment, he simply looked at her, drinking in the sight. "I could look at you forever and not get tired of it."

Claire chuckled softly and blushed. "You don't have to say that."

He leaned over her. "It's true." Then he lowered his head to her breasts and licked his tongue over one nipple.

A strangled moan came from her lips, and her body arched toward him.

"Just like I guessed," he whispered against her warm flesh. "Perfect."

Then he captured the nipple between his lips and sucked on it, while he palmed her other breast and kneaded it until she was writhing underneath him, her arousal now permeating the air around him. She tasted young and pure, so unspoiled he almost forgot what life had in store for her. But he didn't want to think of it, not now, not when he wanted to give her more pleasure than she'd had in her entire life.

This night was for Claire, even though he knew he would get his fair share of pleasure, too. Just watching the way her body moved and her heart beat against her ribcage filled his heart with pride—and his cock with more blood, making him as hard as the rocks the surf was crashing against.

The moonlight bathed her in a warm light, the way sunlight could never achieve. It lent her face an almost mystical glow as if she wasn't real and only a figment of his imagination. And maybe she was; maybe he was dreaming in order to try to escape the monotony of his long life. It didn't matter, because what he sensed underneath his roaming hands felt real: warm flesh, smooth skin, hot blood. She was the personification of perfection.

As he continued to lavish her breasts with kisses and caresses, his hand moved lower, stroking along her torso until he reached her panties. He slid his fingers between fabric and skin, exploring the coarse hair that guarded her sex.

A hitched breath escaped from Claire's lips as he moved lower, but at the same time her hips tilted toward him in invitation.

"Yes, darling, I'm here," he encouraged her and slipped lower, encountering warm and moist flesh that felt as smooth as silk. He bathed his fingers in her arousal, coating them with it before he moved back north.

"Oh, God!" she called out.

His experienced fingers found the tiny swollen organ that lay protected by a hood. He pulled the hood up, exposing her clit fully and slid one moist finger over it. Claire nearly leapt off the ground, her heartbeat accelerating in the same instant.

His own body heated when the scent of her arousal grew stronger. His cock pressed against her thigh, impatiently waiting to get its turn. But it would have to wait a little while longer.

With slow and steady movements, he circled the swollen bundle of nerves underneath his fingers. He kept his touch light, savoring the moment. She was at his mercy now. With his touch, he could command her body and give her pleasure. There would be no escape for her now. No turning back.

"For tonight you'll be mine," he murmured against her breasts. And he would take everything she was willing to give him—and more, he realized that too now. Because she had awakened not just the desire for sex in him, but a darker desire. One she would not freely agree to.

Suddenly impatient, he pulled his hand from her sex and gripped her panties. With one rapid movement, he ripped them off her.

"Fuck it," he cursed and lowered himself between her legs, spreading them wider before lowering his head to her glistening pussy. He slung her legs over his shoulders, one to each side of his head and sunk his mouth onto her.

Surprised gasps echoed through the night. "Jake, oh my God!" she cried out. "You don't have to…"

But her voice died when his tongue lapped over her slit, gathering her arousal. Her taste was intoxicating and invigorating at the same time. He sucked, nibbled, and licked, leaving no spot unexplored. She was beautiful in every way. Her body welcomed him and opened up to his caresses, to his tender ministrations as he now stroked his tongue over her clit and lavished it with gentle touches.

He loved the way she responded to him, the way she lay in front of him, spread out for him to do with as he pleased. His own excitement rose when he felt her body tense and press against him with more urgency. The sounds of pleasure coming from her intensified and spurred him on to give her more. Without removing his lips and tongue from her clit, he brought his hand to her sex and stroked against her soft folds. He extended his middle finger and probed, easing it into her with one continuous slow thrust.

Her muscles clamped around him tightly—more tightly than he would have expected. How long had it been since a man had touched her there? Since a man had driven his cock into her? The thought that nobody had done so in a long time, made him even more impatient to seat himself in her clenching pussy.

"Yes," she moaned. "Oh please yes."

Claire begging for it nearly made him spill. Fuck! He couldn't hold back much longer if she continued like that.

Driving his finger harder into her, he sucked her clit deeper into his mouth and pressed his lips together. Her body erupted, the waves of her orgasm ripping through her and crashing against his lips. Her interior muscles spasmed around his finger, gripping him so firmly that he thought she'd never release him. Not that he would have cared. He loved being inside her.

It took minutes for her body to still and for Jake to remove his lips from her sweet sex. When he did so and looked at her, her eyes were closed. She breathed heavily.

"I've gotta be inside you now," he told her and positioned himself between her legs, bringing his cock to her center.

Claire's eyes opened slowly and a soft smile played around her lips. "Yes," she whispered breathlessly. "Let me feel you."

"You've made me so hard," he pressed out between clenched teeth, barely able to prevent his fangs from descending. His hunger was pushing to the forefront now.

Unable to slow himself down, he thrust inside her with one powerful move, robbing her of the air in her lungs. As she took a breath, her eyes widened.

"Oh my god, you're big. Even bigger than earlier."

Most vampires were. Sex was part and parcel of who they were, and once turned, their vampire blood ensured their cocks were hard and big to pleasure their female partners and give them what they needed. With every stroke he became harder. Coated in her juices and submerged in her body, everything male in him surged to life.

Claire's eyes rolled back and her mouth dropped open, her nipples turning into hard points once more. "Oh God!" she mumbled.

"I told you, you'll feel more than just alive." He smiled down at her and continued to drive in and out of her, increasing his speed. His body found its own rhythm, fucking her hard and fast. He pulled her legs up, spreading her wider in the process, plunging deeper. Her pussy gripped him even tighter now. On her face, he saw the signs of pure pleasure. Her skin took on a healthy tone now, making her look even more beautiful.

He wished he could have gone on forever, but her channel was clenching around him, and the scent of her arousal almost drove him insane with lust. Knowing she was as close as he, he increased his tempo and let himself go.

He felt the rush of his semen through his cock just as her interior muscles spasmed as her orgasm broke. He joined her, thrusting into oblivion with one last stroke, spilling inside her.

Breathing heavily, he dropped his head to the crook of her neck. "You're perfect," he repeated once more and kissed her neck only to realize that his fangs had descended.

He knew what his vampire side demanded from him now. And he couldn't deny himself what he'd craved ever since he'd first touched her: her blood.

"Claire," he said softly, whispering into her ear. "I can't stop."

He licked over the plump vein in her neck and peeled his lips back from his teeth. When his fangs touched her smooth skin, he sensed her shiver beneath him.

Using his suggestive powers, powers every vampire possessed, he sent his thoughts to her.

Feel my kiss. Feel my lips caress you, my tongue lick you.

Then he sank his fangs into her neck and pierced her vein. Rich blood ran over his tongue and down his throat, revitalizing his body. All the while Claire was fully conscious and aware of everything around her—his cock gently thrusting into her, his hands caressing her—except for one thing: she believed that he was kissing her neck, not biting her.

Claire moaned softly.

"Yes. Take from me," she murmured.

Shock coursed through him. Was she aware of what he was doing? Or was she merely drowning in the wave of sexual bliss that his bite was heightening?

Could she feel him? Damn it, he *wanted* her to feel him. To know he was drinking her blood, though he knew it wasn't wise. He wanted her to know what he was: a creature of the night, a man who thirsted for human blood; a vampire.

He sent a question into her mind. *Claire, do you like what I'm doing?* He sucked harder on her vein while he thrust in and out of her sex.

"More…"

Yes, darling, I'll give you more.

Because he wanted more, too. More of Claire.

5

Claire had woken in her own bed, alone, her body still humming from a night of lovemaking with Jake. To her surprise, she wore her nightgown. For a moment she lay there, daydreaming. She felt no regret having given herself to a stranger she'd met only hours earlier. In fact, it had been liberating to be with a man who knew nothing about her. She could just pretend to be who she wanted to be: a young woman who had her life ahead of her.

She couldn't remember how she'd gotten back to her room. And she'd had strange dreams: of Jake biting her neck while he made love to her the second time. She'd enjoyed it, loved the way it had made her feel. She shook her head at the strange notion and got out of bed.

Instantly she swayed, her head suddenly pounding. A sharp stab of pain radiated through her. "Oh God, no!" she whimpered. Another attack was imminent. She searched her room for her handbag and found it sitting on a chair. She rushed to it and opened it, rummaging through it, trying to find her pills. But she couldn't see them. Frantically she spilled the contents of her bag onto the bed, but her pill bottle was not among them.

Another stab of pain assaulted her. She gripped the bed frame for support, waiting for the wave to pass. Then she ran to the door. She had to get Mrs. Adams to call the doctor who she'd seen a few days earlier.

As she grabbed the door knob, her eyes fell onto the dresser next to it. On it stood her pill bottle, a neatly written note underneath it.

I found it in the hallway, it said on stationary belonging to Sunseekers Inn.

Relieved, she snatched the bottle, twisted its top off and popped two pills into her mouth. She swallowed them down with the last swig of the water from the bottle that stood on her nightstand.

Her heart beat frantically now, and none of the bliss she'd felt last night was left. Her illness was encroaching further and further into her life, trying to wipe out any joy she had.

She didn't want to wither away and have the last image of her life be that of excruciating pain. No, the thing she wanted to remember was the pleasure she'd felt when making love to Jake. She wouldn't allow her illness to overshadow that. That's why she had to take charge of her life—or rather, her death.

She'd never truly believed in the power of the hot spring. She'd lied to herself, not wanting to confront the inevitable. But now she was strong enough. She'd felt something beautiful the night before, and she wanted to leave this world while this memory was still strong in her mind. For a few hours she'd been happy. It was all she could have hoped for.

Ignoring the pain in her head she set her bag on the bed and started packing, even though where she was going, she couldn't take anything with her.

~ ~ ~

Jake woke from an uneasy sleep. During the entire day, he'd drifted in and out of sleep, which was unusual for him. But the events of the previous night had shaken him. His mind couldn't rest; it was working overtime. It wasn't fair that Claire should die so young, when he was contemplating taking his own life. How ironic was that? She wanted to live and would die, whereas he wanted to die and would live forever. Life was cruel.

Last night he'd felt needed for the first time in his life. Needed by another person. He'd been able to give Claire pleasure and make her feel desired because he desired her. More than he'd desired any other woman before. Was it because he wanted to save her? Or was it more? Had he finally met a woman who could give him the purpose in his life that he so desperately craved? Had he found somebody to take care of, somebody to give his soul to?

And what about the reason that had brought him to the island? If the hot spring really had any powers, then why wasn't it granting Claire's wish? Or did it indeed need a sacrifice, one that *he* could make?

He had to speak to Claire. After last night he felt close to her, and he hoped she felt the same. If she did, there was something he could offer her. But it had to be her choice.

Impatient for the sun to set, Jake took a shower and got dressed. As soon as the sun dipped below the horizon, he tore out of his room and headed for Claire's. He knocked at the door, but there was no answer. He tried the door knob and it turned. When he looked inside the room, he jerked back involuntarily: the bed was made and the room was empty. All of Claire's personal effects were gone.

Panicked, he rushed downstairs and found Mrs. Adams behind the reception counter.

"Miss Culver, where is she?" he asked without as much as a greeting.

Mrs. Adams raised her eyebrows and gave him a curious look. "She checked out."

His heart stopped. "Where did she go?"

"I don't know."

"What did she say to you? She must have said something." He didn't care that he sounded desperate.

Mrs. Adams frowned. "Now that you're asking. Well, hmm, she said she was ready to leave now. When I asked her where she was heading, she just said *where there is no pain.*"

His heart clenched. "And you didn't stop her?" But he didn't wait for her answer and instead charged out of the house.

Jake stared into the night. Where would she go to end it all? Where would he go? For a moment he let his mind travel, then he could see the place where he would go to end his life: the last place where he'd been happy.

He ran as fast as he could, not caring if anybody saw him and wondered how a man could run as fast as a car. He had to get to Claire. His legs carried him to the beach where they'd made love the night before. He passed the shed, his eyes scanning the shore, when he perceived a movement, where the waves crashed against a small outcropping of rocks.

Claire stood there at the ledge, looking into the distance.

"Claire!" he screamed, but she didn't turn her head. She probably couldn't hear him over the surf that had already drenched her clothes.

He sprinted toward the rocks, his feet sinking into the wet sand with every forceful step. But he didn't let this slow him down. He knew he had to reach her, because her intention was evident from the way she leaned toward the waves. Any second now, she would jump, and the surf would swallow her up and slam her against the rocks.

He couldn't let it happen. And suddenly he knew that there was a way for both of them to get their wish. As he ran toward her and raced up the rocks, he finally realized what his heart's true desire was. It wasn't to be mortal again; it was to regain his humanity, to feel needed, to feel loved. Claire was the key. That's why he was here. Not for the magical spring, but to save her.

And he couldn't fail now. Not when he was so close. Not when so much was at stake.

As he reached the top of the rocks, another big wave crashed, hitting Claire.

He stretched out his arms, barreling toward her, but the wave swept her up, made her lose her footing.

"Nooooooo!" The scream dislodged from his throat as he lunged for her with superhuman strength and speed. His fingers found purchase, wrapping around her arm. He pulled her from the clutches of the dark ocean, dragging her toward him, holding her tightly to him, as the next wave already built. But by the time it crashed against the rocks, he'd already carried Claire to safety.

She seemed dazed in his arms as he carried her to the beach and brought them down in the dry sand. Finally, relief flooded him, and he dared breathe again.

A sob tore from her. "Why didn't you let me die, Jake?"

"Shh, darling," he cooed.

She struggled in his arms, pushing against him. "I have brain cancer. I can't take the pain any longer…"

He drew her closer to his chest and stroked his palm over her wet hair, feeling her shiver. "I know, darling."

She braced her hands against his chest, pushing him. "You knew?"

"I found your pill bottle. Mrs. Adams told me the rest."

Another sob tore from her chest. "Is that why you slept with me? Because you pitied me?"

"No! I made love to you because I desire you. I want you more than anything else in this life." It was the truth, though he had no idea how it had happened. Maybe it was fate. Or maybe it was the magical spring.

More tears streamed over her cheeks. With his thumb he wiped them away.

"Claire, what I tell you now might seem fantastic, but it's the truth. Do you think you can keep an open mind?"

"About what?"

"You want to live, don't you?"

A sob bigger than the previous one disturbed the night.

"Then I have a solution for you. The spring worked, Claire. Because it brought us together. You've wished for a cure. I can give you one."

Her big blue eyes stared at him, half in hope, half in doubt. "How?"

"I'm a vampire, Claire, I'm immortal, and I can give you immortality."

He watched her eyes as her expression changed to disbelief. "No." She shook her head and pulled back. "No."

"It's true. And you know it. Deep down you know, don't you?" He focused his gaze on the spot on her neck where he'd bitten her the night before.

Her hand came up to touch that same spot.

"You know it because you felt it last night. You sensed my bite."

Her lips parted as if she wanted to say something, but nothing came out. Then she stroked over her neck. "I dreamed it."

"It wasn't a dream. When I made love to you the second time, I used my suggestive powers to make you believe my bite was just a kiss. But I think I didn't use my powers to their full extent, because deep down I wanted you to know what I was doing."

Slowly, realization seemed to settle in. "You drank my blood."

He nodded and put his hand on her neck, brushing over the bite mark. Only he and other vampires could see it. To humans, the mark was invisible. "And I loved it. Let me give you something in return. Let me help you."

"How?" she whispered and looked straight at him.

"I can turn you into a vampire. It will wipe out any illness or disease you have. You'll be immortal and without pain."

"Immortal? And how would I live? In the dark? Drinking blood?" Her lips trembled.

"The dark can be beautiful." He pointed to the canopy of stars in the night sky. "Even in the dark there's light, there's beauty."

"And the blood?" she whispered.

"There are ways. You wouldn't have to feed directly from humans if you didn't want to. Though you might grow to like it. But if you don't, there are always blood banks."

She looked at him for a long while, clearly contemplating his words. "I'm scared."

Jake reached for her, stroking his knuckles over her cheek. "I know. But I'll be here for you."

Slowly she moved her head closer. "Why would you do that for me? Didn't you come here with a wish, too?"

He smiled. "Do you know what I wished for?"

She shook her head.

"To be mortal again." He sighed. "But I understand now that it wasn't my heart's true desire. It wasn't my mortality I wanted."

"How do you know that?"

"I know because I'm holding my heart's true desire in my arms right now. I know now that I was drawn to this island so I could meet you and fulfill your wish."

"So the spring really does work?"

He kissed her. "Yes. But only for those who are prepared to open their eyes and trust in the impossible. So, Claire, do you trust me to give you a second life?"

Slowly, she nodded. "I trust you. I don't know why, but I do."

"It won't hurt," he promised. "I'll drain you of your human blood, and at your last heartbeat, I'll feed you mine. When you wake, you'll be like me, a creature of the night."

"What if it doesn't work?"

"I promise you it will work."

She swallowed and her voice trembled when she spoke her next words. "When I wake, will you be there?" Her eyes glimmered with hope.

"Claire, I want a life with you. If you want that, too, I'll be there for you through eternity as your lover. If you don't, I'll be by your side as your friend. The choice is yours."

There was no hesitation in her voice when she responded to him. "Bite me, my lover." She closed her eyes and whispered again, "My lover for eternity."

His heart jumping with joy, he lowered his lips to her neck and pierced her skin with his fangs. He sucked on the plump vein, feeling Claire shiver. To reassure her that she would be safe, he caressed her tenderly and sent his thoughts to her.

Easy, darling. All will be fine soon. Trust me. I'll keep you safe.

The more blood he took from her, the more her heartbeat slowed. His own heart beat faster now. It had been a long time since he'd turned a human, and the process wasn't without risk. If he gave her his blood too early, the turning wouldn't take and she would die suffering excruciating pain. Equally, if he waited too long, she would die, though it would be as if she merely fell asleep. Neither of those two scenarios was acceptable. He needed for Claire to live. He'd promised her.

I'll keep you safe, he repeated once more and removed his fangs from her neck, then pierced his own wrist. Blood dripped from it.

"Now," he murmured to himself.

6

The darkness around her was suddenly retreating, making space for warmth and light. She wasn't sure what the source of the light was, but she could feel it shine against her closed lids. Around her was softness. Her ears picked up different sounds, some distant, some close by. Her gums itched, and involuntarily, she ground her teeth.

The fog that had been her constant companion for the last year and the pain that had overshadowed her life were gone. In its stead she felt strength and power, an energy that seemed unreal. Even before her illness she'd never felt like this.

"Claire."

The sound of her name being spoken drifted to her. As if somebody was calling her to leave the beautiful dream world she was in. She didn't want to listen to it, didn't want to leave the place where she felt no pain.

"Claire, stay with me."

She recognized that voice. Jake's voice. Her lover from the night before. A stranger, yet she'd never felt closer to anyone.

Her lips parted to speak, and only then did she realize that she hadn't been breathing. Air rushed into her lungs, filling them, expanding them. A gasp escaped on her first exhale. Her eyes flew open at the same time. While she tried to focus them, memories rushed back. Memories of her body being drained of blood, of her heartbeat slowing. Memories of her getting a new life. A second chance.

"I'm alive," she murmured, glancing around. She wasn't at the beach anymore. She lay on a bed, naked beneath the sheets. The shutters of the window were closed, but she could tell that it was daylight outside.

Jake sat at the edge of the bed. "Yes, alive and immortal." His impossibly blue eyes pinned her, his lips curving into a smile. "I brought you to my room." He gently brushed a strand of her hair from her forehead. "I undressed and bathed you. You were soaked." He motioned to his own nude torso and the towel that was wrapped around his lower half. "And so was I."

She nodded and raised her hand to touch his chest. Beneath her fingers sparks seemed to ignite. Surprised, she met his eyes. "You feel different."

He captured her hand and pressed it to the spot where his heart beat, steady and strong. "All your senses are more pronounced now. Everything you touch feels more real, more intense. Everything you see is sharper, the colors more vibrant. Your sense of smell is better than any animal's, your hearing more sensitive than ever."

She could feel everything he was describing. And more. Slowly, she ran her hand down his torso, until her fingers brushed up against the towel. "And my appetite for sex?"

Jake bent closer, a seductive smile playing around his lips. "More insatiable than you can imagine." He winked. "But I'm happy to oblige."

He took her hand and pressed it against the towel. Beneath it, she felt the hard outline of his cock.

"Mmm." She squeezed his erection and felt her clit throb in response. "I need to feel you."

She licked her lips and felt her gums itch at the same time. Taking a hasty breath, she opened her mouth wider. She sensed her fangs descending.

"Beautiful." Jake's eyes darkened and he stroked his index finger over her lips, before rubbing it over one fang.

A bolt of energy charged through her, and she gasped. Never had she felt anything as intensely as Jake touching her there. "Oh God! What's happening?"

He moved closer, his lips now only inches from her mouth. "Fangs are a vampire's most erogenous zone. Touching you there, licking you there, will feel to you as if I were touching and licking your pussy. I can make you come just by licking your fangs." And judging by the glint in his eyes, he wanted to do just that.

The thought aroused her, made all kinds of wanton ideas swamp her mind. Was this what it meant to be a vampire? To be ruled by ones desires, ones basest instincts? More than one of those instincts reared its head already. She swallowed hard.

"I'm..." She didn't know how to express what she needed.

"Thirsty? I know. It's natural. I have human blood for you." He pointed to a bag in a corner of the room. "But first..." He locked eyes with hers. "I want the first blood you drink to be mine. I want you to remember your first bite as something beautiful."

Her eyes widened. "Bite *you*? Another vampire?"

"Yes. It's common among lovers. It heightens the pleasure. And you wanted me as your lover, didn't you? Or did you change your mind?" A flicker of uncertainty appeared in his mesmerizing eyes.

She hastened to dispel his doubts, cupping his cheek. "I want you." She dropped her gaze to the artery that pulsed at his neck and ran her finger over the tempting spot. What would it feel like to bite him and drink his blood?

A second later, Jake tossed the towel to the floor, revealing his erect cock, and pulled back the duvet. He ran his eyes over her naked body, and the admiration and desire in them made her heart beat faster. She reached for him, pulled him down to her.

Surprised at her own strength, she smiled. "I think I'm going to like this."

Tenderly he caressed her neck, trailing his fingers along her pulsing vein. "As will I. Now that you're as strong as I, I won't have to be careful anymore not to hurt you. When I took you the night on the beach, I had to hold back."

"It didn't feel like you were holding back."

He chuckled. "You've seen nothing yet."

At the thought of making love to Jake, she felt a shudder race through her, while butterflies seemed to swirl in her stomach. "Then show me. I want to experience everything. I want to live fully now. Without holding back."

"Anything you want, darling."

He nudged his cock at her center. The contact of hard male flesh to soft female flesh was more electrifying than the first time. Every nerve ending in her body seemed to be on overdrive, sending impressions back to her brain, sensations that were so intense she could hardly believe they were her own.

Claire spread her legs wider, making space to accommodate him, and he didn't lose any time and plunged into her to the hilt. She welcomed the forceful invasion with a moan, loving the way he filled her. While she'd always been one to enjoy slow and gentle lovemaking, she had the feeling that she would very quickly get addicted to the wild and passionate sex Jake was promising.

There was nothing hesitant or slow about the way he thrust into her, his cock impaling her. Deep and hard. Powerful and fast. Relentless. She wrapped her legs around him, her ankles locking below his butt, and every time he drove into her, she pulled him deeper, demanding he give her more.

His eyes pinned her, a red rim around his irises, an orange glow spreading. His lips were parted, showing the tips of his fangs, and by God, how the sight turned her on. He was all vampire now. Powerful, immortal, and all hers.

"Bite me," he murmured, tilting his head to the side and bringing his neck to her lips. "Taste me." He rocked harder into her and growled. "And later, when you're exhausted from your orgasms, I'll fuck your pretty mouth."

The erotic image snapped the last thread of her self-control. Her fangs extended to their full length, and even if she'd wanted to, she wouldn't have been able to stop her next action. She set her fangs at the spot where his neck and shoulder connected and licked over the glistening skin. The salty taste only heightened her thirst, and she pierced his vein with the sharp tips, lodging them deep in his flesh. If he tried to move away, her sharp canines would rip his flesh, but Jake didn't jerk back. Instead, he plunged his cock deeper, just as she pulled on his vein and took her first conscious taste of his blood. Though he'd turned her by giving her his blood, she had no memory of it.

This was her first true taste of Jake. His blood was rich and thick; its taste sent a thrill into every cell of her body, awakening everything that was female and vampire in her. She sucked harder, needing more of this addicting elixir he so freely offered.

"Fuck!" he ground out and shuddered. "It's too good!"

She felt him spasm inside her, flooding her with his essence, but still he didn't slow down, didn't stop his relentless thrusts. He shifted his angle and continued, his cock just as hard as before his orgasm, while she swallowed his blood and let it permeate her body, sending a tingling through all her cells.

Her orgasm came without any preamble, simply hit her out of nowhere and swallowed her like an ocean wave. Gasping, she pulled her fangs from Jake's neck, her body spasming.

"Yes, that's it, darling!" he praised and rocked inside her a few more times, before he pulled out of her.

Before disappointment about the abrupt end to their lovemaking had time to spread, he'd already rolled her onto her stomach and pulled her ass up in the air. A second later, he was back inside her, his impossibly hard cock fucking her from behind.

She cried out in pleasure and surprise. "Jake!"

"I told you I wouldn't hold back." He gripped her hips tightly and slammed into her.

"But you already came," she managed to say, lifting herself onto her elbows.

"I drank pints of your blood. I'm going to be hard for a very long time, no matter how many orgasms I have."

The revelation made the fire in her belly burn even brighter. Her vampire lover would make love to her until they both couldn't move another limb. And right now, he was taking her so hard, plowing into her from behind, that a human woman would have screamed in agony. Yet, she, Claire Culver, newly turned vampire, welcomed every thrust of his hard cock into her soft center, craving more the more Jake gave her.

"Fuck me, Jake!" she cried out, not caring if anybody in the Bed and Breakfast could hear them.

He pounded into her, gripping her so tightly that despite her new vampire strength she wouldn't have been able to escape him.

"Did you like my blood?" he asked breathlessly, his voice a mere growl now.

"I loved it." It was the truth.

"Good."

As if he wanted to thank her for her answer, he slipped one hand to her front and found her clit with unerring precision. He rubbed his moist finger over it, once, twice, and she erupted once more. An orgasm more powerful than the first washed over her. Jake shuddered at the same time, more of his semen spilling inside her, lubricating her channel even more.

"Fuck, yeah!" he groaned and slowed, while her pussy still quivered with aftershocks.

~ ~ ~

Still shaking from his second orgasm, Jake pulled from her sheath. He couldn't get enough of Claire. But he didn't want to steamroll her either. He had to assure himself that she really wanted this, that she really like being fucked like this. After all, there was no way she could have guessed how wild he'd get in bed, and how insatiable he truly was.

Gently, he turned her back onto her back. Her eyes gleamed with satisfaction, her heartbeat raced, and her skin glistened with sweat. She reached for him. He bent down to her and kissed her, tenderly at first, but within seconds, the kiss turned heated. With a moan, he ripped his lips from her.

"God, Claire, you're driving me insane." He shoved a hand through his damp hair and threw his head back. "The things I want to do to you... How I want to take you, make you mine..." He sighed. "If you don't stop me, I'm going to take you every which way I can. And I mean *every*. So you'd better put the brakes on, or I can't guarantee what'll happen."

Her eyes turned molten. By God, she was all vampire, through and through. Down to the insatiable lust for sex. He'd done that to her. But had she really wanted this? Had she truly chosen this?

She opened her eyes wider, her lashes crashing against her brows, a motion so seductive, it robbed him of his breath. Her tongue emerged, licking over her lower lip. She knew exactly how she was tempting him. Luring him.

"That night at the beach," she murmured, her hand sliding down to his ass. "When you bit me while you made love to me the second time, I could feel that you wanted to take me harder, but you restrained yourself."

"You made me so wild, your blood... it only added to my desire for you."

"It felt good. All of it. The bite; your cock inside me; feeling that you wanted me."

"I still want you. Now even more."

"Then take me any way you want to, because I want the same. I want to experience everything with you. No holding back."

"A woman after my own heart." He lifted himself off her and got out of bed, pulling her with him.

"What are you doing?"

He led her toward the bathroom. "I want to shower with you, and then I want you on your knees in front of me, sucking my cock as if it's the best thing you've ever had."

When her eyes started to glow only the way a vampire's could, his heart jumped with joy.

"Under one condition."

He froze. "Condition?" He wasn't used to a woman making demands.

Claire molded her luscious body to his, bringing her mouth to his ear. "Don't pull out before I'm done with you. I don't want to spill a single drop."

He sandwiched her between his body and the door frame. "God, woman! What are you trying to do to me?"

"I just want to please you."

He sank his hungry mouth onto hers, silencing her so she couldn't utter any more seductive words, while he lifted her up and slid her onto his cock. He took her right there against the wall until another orgasm had calmed him enough so he could proceed with his original plan of watching Claire kneel in front of him, his cock in her beautiful mouth, while he thrust back and forth, claiming one more part of her.

7

Three months later – New York City

Jake cursed and slammed the guy into the wall next to a dumpster, noticing from the corner of his eye how Claire was already taking care of the young woman the man had attacked and clearly planned to rape.

No matter how often he and Claire roamed the streets of Manhatten at night, there seemed to be an endless supply of criminals. But even though at first he'd vowed not to get involved in humans' problems, one look at Claire's pleading face, and he knew that he couldn't deny her anything. God, how he'd grown to love this woman. It was time to tell her just how much.

"You know we have to help them," she'd said shortly after their arrival in New York, when they'd come upon a man robbing an elderly couple at gunpoint. "If we don't do it, who will?"

Who indeed?

So he'd given in. And—grudgingly—he had to admit to himself that he liked helping people, saving those who couldn't save themselves. And the more humans he and Claire saved the more of his humanity he seemed to regain. The goodness in Claire's heart was contagious, and she'd clearly infected him with it. Though there was no way in hell he'd admit it to anybody. After all, who'd ever heard of a nice vampire?

"She's hurt," Claire advised him now, while she tried to calm the scared woman.

"Heal her."

In the meantime, he'd take care of the jerk, who was now getting back onto his feet and turning around, fists at the ready. Jake grunted with satisfaction. He loved beating up assholes, and when they tried to put up a fight, it was even more fun. And most of the time he didn't even use his vampire powers to exact punishment. He got more satisfaction out of it when he traded kicks and blows with his opponent and let him believe—if only for a while—that they were matched in strength.

Jake slammed his fist into the guy's face, hearing the bones in his nose break. A cry of pain echoed through the night, and the scent of blood permeated the air in the dark alley. Involuntarily, his fangs lengthened and he didn't bother hiding them from the human. The jerk deserved to feel fear.

Jake glared at his opponent, peeling back his lips from his gums to give him a good view of his deadly canines.

"Fuck!" the man croaked and stumbled backward.

Jake tilted his head to the side. "Yeah, you could say that." Slowly, he crossed the distance, pulled his arm back and landed a blow in the guy's gut, making him nearly fold in half.

"No! Please," he whimpered. "Don't kill me!"

He had no intention of killing him. It wouldn't be punishment for what he'd done to the young woman. How he'd scared her.

Jake pressed the guy against the wall and brought his face to within a few inches of his, fangs extended. "Not tonight. But you touch another woman, you as much as look at one, I'm going to rip you to shreds." He snarled, pausing to let the sound echo off the walls. "I'll be watching you. You're not safe from me anywhere. Know that. One false move, and I'll be hunting you like an animal."

The man trembled with fear. He fairly smelled of it.

"You understand?"

Teeth chattering, he managed to nod.

"Good. As for your goodbye present…"

Jake pounded into the despicable human, breaking his jaw and bloodying his eyes, before he kicked him toward the exit of the alley. "Run if you want to live."

He watched with satisfaction as the injured assailant staggered toward the next street. When he turned a corner, Jake retracted his fangs. Then he pivoted and marched to where Claire was taking care of the young woman.

He crouched down next to them and quickly assessed the human's injuries. She had lacerations on her arms and hands, as well as her neck and face. But the wounds weren't deep. The shock and fear were clearly the bigger problem.

But it appeared that Claire was already taking care of that, because the victim's eyes appeared to be focusing on nothing, as if she were in a trance.

"You're using mind control?"

Claire looked at him for a moment. "Just like you taught me. Her injuries aren't severe, but I don't want her to have those memories."

He nodded. "I agree."

Claire looked back at the woman and concentrated on her. He watched her, noticing how calm and self-assured she was. As she sent her thoughts into the woman's mind, erasing the memory of the attack, he noticed Claire's fingernails turn into claws. Beautiful, deadly claws. Claws with which she left deep cuts in his back whenever they made love. Just thinking of it made him hard.

"She's ready," Claire announced and punctured the pad of her index finger with her claw, before bringing the bleeding finger to the young woman's lips, making her drink from it.

While she fed the human the vampire blood, she looked over her shoulder. "I'm still fascinated with the healing power of our blood. Can you imagine the illnesses and injuries we could heal?"

He shook his head lightly. Leave it to Claire to be the Good Samaritan. "If humans knew of our existence and what our blood is capable of, they'd hunt us to the ends of the earth."

Claire motioned to the exit of the alley. "You didn't wipe that man's memory. What makes you think he won't tell everybody that he was attacked by a vampire?"

"He's too busy peeing into his pants and looking over his shoulder to breathe a word about what happened here tonight. I know his type. Preying on the weak. He won't talk."

"No, he won't. I made sure of that."

Jake jumped up, whirling around at the same time, his hand already inside his jacket, pulling out his stake. Adrenaline was pumping through him—because the man who'd spoken was without a doubt a vampire.

Silhouetted against the lights from the main street, the stranger stood at the entrance to the alley. Instinctively, Jake braced himself. He was not only responsible for protecting Claire, but also the young human in their temporary care.

The stranger moved toward him with a steady gait. As he came closer, Jake squared his stance, readying himself for the fight. And there would be a fight, no doubt. Because now that he could see his face, he knew this man was no pushover: while the ponytail of long dark-brown hair might have given the impression that he was a laid-back guy, the long scar that reached from his left ear to his chin gave an altogether different one. This vampire wouldn't shy away from a fight: his scar suggested that even as a human he'd fought ferociously.

"Get the woman to safety, Claire," he murmured, turning his head slightly.

But Claire had already jumped up. "I'm not leaving your side."

"Damn it, do as I say."

"I'd suggest she stays where she is. The human, too," the vampire coming toward them said, spreading his arms. "My friends can take care of her."

From behind him, two more men appeared, both now walking toward them.

"Shit!" Jake cursed. The one with the scar he could have defeated, but two more? Were he alone, he wouldn't hesitate, but he had to consider Claire's safety, as well as that of the human woman.

He lifted his chin. "You and your friends killed the human?"

One side of the scarred vampire's lip curled up in a sneer. "Do I look like I kill for pleasure?"

"You do." As did the other two, whose faces he could see clearly now.

Both men were tall. While the one on the left was skinny and bald and had an evil sneer on his face, the other was built like a tank and wore his black hair down to his shoulders.

The tank chuckled. "Gabriel, you shouldn't ask questions like that. You're just spooking the guy."

Gabriel, the scarred one, tossed a quick look over his shoulder. "Shut it, Amaury. Let's get down to business."

"I'll take care of the human," the bald vampire offered.

Amaury, the tank, lifted an eyebrow. "Really, Zane?" He shook his head, grinning. "You're just gonna scare the shit out of her. You have no sensitivity when it comes to women. I'm better at that."

"Nobody touches the human," Jake growled, taking a step toward the three men. "She's under my protection."

"And under mine!" Claire piped up, moving shoulder-to-shoulder with him.

"Damn it, Claire!" Couldn't this woman listen for once and get herself to safety like he'd asked her to?

"Looks like he can't even control his own woman," Zane, the bald one, commented. "Gabriel, you sure about this?"

"I'm sure." Gabriel ran his eyes over Claire then back to him. "We've been cleaning up after you for the last few nights."

"Cleaning up? You mean killing the criminals I was teaching a lesson?"

"I didn't say that." Gabriel, who clearly was the leader of the three, exchanged looks with his two cohorts. "Since you didn't find it necessary to wipe their memories, I did it for you. And it's getting a little annoying. So we figured we'd bring you in. Make you aware of the rules."

"Bring me in?" Jake's jaw set into a grim line. "Over my fucking charred body."

"Definitely stubborn," Amaury threw in. "I like him."

Forehead furrowed, Jake tossed him a look. "Yeah, well, I don't like you. None of you."

"What a shame," Zane grunted, "and there I thought we'd become best buddies."

"Not likely!" He doubted that Zane was capable of friendship. The guy gave off an air of pure evil.

"Maybe we started off on the wrong foot," Gabriel said calmly. "I believe introductions are in order. I'm Gabriel Giles." He motioned to the tank. "Meet my colleagues: Amaury—" Then he pointed to the bald one. "—and Zane. We're bodyguards."

"Bodyguards? You're shitting me." Who'd ever heard of vampires being bodyguards?

Gabriel nodded. "We work for a company called Scanguards."

Jake shrugged. "Never heard of it."

"That's how it's supposed to be. We don't exactly advertise our services."

Getting impatient, Jake asked, "What do you want?"

Gabriel tilted his head toward the human. Instantly Jake lifted his hand, gripping the stake tighter, and growled.

"Quick temper," Zane tossed in. "I like that."

Gabriel ignored his colleague's comment and made a calming hand movement. "You misunderstand me. I don't want the human. But I like that you're protecting her. Just like you and your woman have been helping other humans. That's why I want to talk to you."

"It's a trick, isn't it? You want me to relax so you can kill me and Claire and then kill the human."

Gabriel shook his head.

"Not the brightest bulb in the shed," Zane grunted.

Gabriel tossed him an annoyed glance. "You're not helping."

"Didn't think I was supposed to."

"Excuse my associate. I'm afraid Zane has a hard time accepting new people we want to hire into the company."

Had he heard correctly? "Hire?"

"Yes. We can't handle the increasing workload with the number of bodyguards we currently have. Samson, our boss has tasked us with recruiting more likeminded vampires."

Could this be real? "Likeminded?" he found himself asking.

Amaury patted Gabriel on the shoulder, grinning. "Yeah, you know, cuddly, fuzzy vampires like us—" At those words he pointed to Zane and Gabriel. "—who make sure crime doesn't get out of hand. We need guys like you to help us protect the innocent." He paused for a moment. "Pays well, too."

Jake exchanged a look with Claire, who appeared just as surprised as he. Then he stared back at the three vampires. "You're here to recruit me?"

Gabriel nodded. "You want the job? You'd get paid for what you're obviously already doing. Patrolling the streets of Manhattan and protecting the innocent. There'll be other assignments, too. We work for politicians, celebrities, anybody who can afford us."

This sounded better and better. He gripped Claire's hand, looking at her. "I work in a team."

"You'll be teamed up with somebody," Gabriel reassured him.

"Claire is my partner. We're a package deal. You hire me. You hire her."

"Just because she's your lover—"

"She's the woman I love," he cut Gabriel off.

Gabriel exchanged a look with his two associates, while Claire tugged at his hand, making him meet her eyes.

"You love me?" she murmured.

He bent closer. "More than my life. And I should have told you so long ago."

Suddenly her arms were around his neck and her lips brushing over his. "I love you, Jake."

He took her lips in a passionate kiss.

"Well, that's just great," Zane grumbled. "You know, Gabriel, if you insist on hiring both, you're gonna have to make a rule that there's no kissing on the job."

Jake let go of Claire's lips and turned back to the three men of Scanguards.

Gabriel met his gaze. "Okay, you both have a job with us, but there'll be rules. Got that?"

"Got it."

"Good, then let's send the human on her way, and we'll take you to Scanguards HQ and introduce you to Samson." Gabriel crossed the distance between them with several long strides, offering his hand. "Welcome to Scanguards, Jake."

Jake shook his hand. Everything in his life was perfect now. Claire loved him and he loved her. And now he would be part of a group of vampires who'd taken it upon themselves to do good.

What could be better than that?

~ ~ ~

ABOUT THE AUTHOR

Tina Folsom was born in Germany and has been living in English speaking countries for over 25 years, the last 15 of them in San Francisco, where she's married to an American.

Tina has always been a bit of a globe trotter: after living in Lausanne, Switzerland, she briefly worked on a cruise ship in the Mediterranean, then lived a year in Munich, before moving to London. There, she became an accountant. But after 8 years she decided to move overseas.

In New York she studied drama at the American Academy of Dramatic Arts, then moved to Los Angeles a year later to pursue studies in screenwriting. This is also where she met her husband, who she followed to San Francisco three months after first meeting him.

In San Francisco, Tina worked as a tax accountant and even opened her own firm, then went into real estate, however, she missed writing. In 2008 she wrote her first romance and never looked back.

She's always loved vampires and decided that vampire and paranormal romance was her calling. She now has over 32 novels in English and dozens in other languages (Spanish, German, and French) and continues to write, as well as have her existing novels translated.

For more about Tina Folsom:

www.tinawritesromance.com
http://www.facebook.com/TinaFolsomFans
Twitter: @Tina_Folsom
Email: tina@tinawritesromance.com

59370741R00078

Made in the USA
San Bernardino, CA
05 December 2017